# That Much Water

a novel

by

## M. P. Ness

End the Madness

**Bolt Publishing, LLC**
478 E. Altamonte Drive Ste 108-782,
Altamonte Springs FL 32701

ISBN:9781987415247

Printed in the United States via Createspace

1 9 2 8 3 7 4 6 5

Publisher Note:

This book is a work of fiction.
All of the names, places,
and events that occur are from
the author's imagination.
Any resemblance to an actual
person, alive or dead, place,
historical event, or business establishment
is purely coincidental.

Contributions:

**M.P. Ness** – Art Designer
**JoAnn Debo** – Editor
**Jeremy Croston** – Content Manager

Obligatory Author's Disclaimer:
*This is a work of fiction based on heinous, self-evident, plausibly deniable, but not-so-well concealed truths in our age.*

*Any resemblance to any existing **person** is so completely coincidental that it would be a miracle such a resemblance could even happen.*
*And yet, such a miracle did happen to come along...in a way.*
*...Fascinating...*

*Other resemblances are, well, they're unfortunate truths concerning the state of our world, and the author does not apologize for, nor regret pointing them out as he sees them. They are not conspiracy, theory, manifesto, nor agenda. They are blatant, obvious, deliberately executed states of being. If whosoever they resemble is implicated and offended by that fact, they should instead be offended by themselves and their own atrocious actions.*

*In fact, the only regret the author possesses pertaining to this work of fiction is an obvious one...*

*...That he didn't complete writing, editing, and publishing sooner...each of which steps take time, and careful crafting.*
*But perhaps now, the social climate the world over is even more appropriate than ever for these words to be seen.*

*And for now... take a look at **us**.*

"We are each of us only comprised of That Much Water..."

*A* man awoke in the high desert.

He spun alert abruptly, spiraling up from the black nothing of a dreamless slumber.

His name was once Adam Penhale.

Today, however, he was no longer Adam. Today, he wasn't much of a man at all; much less a human being.

Amnesic, total and complete, he knew no prior experience, fathomed no dreams, nor suffered any nightmares. He had no past to reference, no memories to recall, nor species, race or personal identity to designate upon himself. He had no hopes, nor aspirations for the future. He was nothing, and thereby nothing existed to muddle his uniqueness in his waking purity. Like a newborn child, he simply, flatly, stirred back to life, a void entity blank as a piece of slate before the artisan's chisel came to craft him.

The arid scent of hot sands filled his nostrils, thick with the taste of earth despite its dryness. The air scalded his sinuses, and seared his skin as a wind blew over his figure, doing nothing to sooth the seething, penetrating blast of the equatorial sun as it burned down through a thoroughly cloudless sky.

The breezy, delicate, desolate sound grazed his right ear, where his left was buried along with half his face in the tiny dune that was slowly drifting in to bury him. It was a grinding on his fresh senses. It built with a swell to him, a ferocious roar despite its lazy movement. He'd never heard anything like it. He'd never heard anything before, so far as he knew, and the sound, so entirely new, was terrifying beyond reason or explanation.

His right eye opened. His left, buried and crusted over with the grains of the earth and salt of his sleep, refused to cooperate, remaining in blackness even as it ached with chafing. But he was none the wiser and considered nothing of it in this first moment of his life.

It was that abrasive sound, not the dangers inherent in the searing of the sun that had awakened him. However, even as confusion and complete unreasonable panic threatened to overcome him, he first experienced a moment of calm.

His buried ear picked up the steady throb of his heartbeat at rest, which seemed to be the very voice of the earth as she churned her forever turning, lulling him, silencing what better judgement might tell another person in his situation.

He didn't have the words to describe what he was feeling. He didn't even have words. He simply was, and oddly, that calm fulfilled him for the moment. He was content to remain exactly as he was, and slip back into an exhausted slumber. But then *instinct* arose, the first and primary designator of life. The confusion roused his waking mind, instilling fear and shaking free the dreamlike moments between the blackness that was and the reality that had come so harshly into focus.

The fear crept into him as his one eye took in the brilliance of the endless blue sky set at right, yet due to gravity's pull, he somehow knew it lay above the glaring golden glow of the sand which warped and shimmered at left in the grips of the sheer heat radiating from its surface.

Such an unfamiliar, alien landscape would have terrified anyone upon first waking; especially those comfortable within their home's familiar surroundings when they'd gone to sleep. But he had no such recollection to reference, and his terror was petrifying and paramount.

With reference, he could have awakened anywhere strange; a hospital after trauma, a bus on his way to some untold routine destination, or even a lounge chair with his favorite book in his lap, and felt a measure of disorientation and possibly, momentary fear. But he had none of this.

He was as a baby, opening his eyes for the first time. And like an infant, he was on the verge of wailing sobs, burdened by the weight of sin inherent in his soul at the dawn of his creation; according to some whom would damn a man before corruption was even possible.

His cry, when it did finally come, was first an incomprehensible babbling scream that rose steadily from within him. A swell of revulsion and instinctual terror, it grew until it became a sound and poured rambling free from his lungs and throat, a ceaseless raw expression fabricated by the sheer experience of every second that passed of the unfamiliar reality his uninitiated consciousness was forced to endure.

It was the gibbering scream of a man gripped in the terror that comes when one realizes he is thoroughly, indisputably, insane. It was the cry of waking consciousness, set reeling as it registered every new shocking detail of its perception; perception it could only recoil from and seek to shut out as it realized that whatever it was, wherever it was, and no matter what had brought it to here and now, it was utterly alone and completely defenseless against the unavoidable, incessant onslaught of what it was to *be.*

He wailed and screamed, and even his own voice terrified him, his sounds jarring in their wild, uncontrolled, and shocking volume. Worse, the sensation of their connection to his innermost parts rattled his fledgling psyche. He thrashed before he knew he could even move, and his flailing became a scramble to get to his feet.

Instinct alone carried him up, but having no recollection of how to do what came so naturally for others, he staggered and collapsed into the powdered earth. Throughout his rise and fall, he screamed. He screeched until his dry throat went hoarse, and he simply knelt there, clutching at himself wildly, wracked with sobs.

His voice seemed to come back at him, but never truly did, for there was simply nothing to rebound his echo. For as far as he could see, in every direction, there was simply nothing but sand, dune after dune after dune, gently undulating waves of shimmering gold unto the horizons far.

The world began to spin, and he wretched and heaved and fell into the sands, unconscious.

So lost, he hadn't even realized that he'd carried something in his left hand through the entire ordeal.

So lost, he hadn't even realized he possessed hands to begin with.

* * *

**When** he woke next, the terror took a different form.

*Darkness.*

Eternal brother to life-giving light, which terrified him first with the harshness of its spectrums, darkness was his world now, and one could about guess at where his ignorance might carry his unreasoning mind.

He came to with a start this time, jolting free of what should have been a nightmare, but wasn't. It wasn't anything. He hadn't dreamed.

Where before, he'd had no reference of past; tonight, he had at least one thing to recall, and due to this, when his eyes opened this time, the terror was infinitely faster in claiming him.

He bolted awake, scrambling up to all fours like an animal, and he scrabbled backward, desperate as a beast seeking to put its back in a corner. He again recoiled in fear from the few things he could see, namely the three-quarter moon as it climbed high, drawing his eyes to the brilliance of the stars in the galaxy as they lit up the night sky.

Gone was the vibrancy of the blue and the sea of gold and all of their swelter. Now all that remained was the dark and her cold lights, an alien landscape to one who was only familiar with a brief, frightening a glimpse of another.

There was no escape, however. No matter how he backed away, there was no respite, as the stars were innumerable beyond count. They were all around; a billion potentially lethal little bugs which he could barely fathom.

Quickly, he brought his eyes down to seek a place to hide, but nothing availed. He was nowhere. His eyes fought to adjust to the dark after being pierced by the heavens, and he hung his head low, cowering from their lofty threat. After all, their piercing look was menacing, and at any moment, those bugs might descend upon him. He had no knowledge of bugs. Instincct alone created them for his fear to feed upon.

He recoiled then as well from the blackness that swept over the dune-scape, making a shifting, uncertain world of unimaginable hunters without name, knowledge, or definition.

It could have been a nightmare, but for the fact that it went on and on, forcing him backward no matter which way he turned.

His fresh mind began to crack, driven mad with his inability to so much as formulate a word-based thought with which to define what his senses were receiving.

For hours, like this, he struggled in vain to hide, and screamed and babbled and blubbered his insane, unfortunate predicament.

It wasn't until late that night when he had his first real, somewhat coherent thought...

He uttered vehement, voiceless, wordless curses upon whatever had brought him here. Whatever it was, whatever he was, and all of wherever this hell was, were yet collectively beyond both he and all of his ability to reason, and so, all he knew was the sensation of *hate*.

Terror was a powerful thing, overwhelmingly encompassing. But it was also thoughtless, a thing which required no reason or mind to truly exist within this man. It simply filled him, forged hatred from nothingness, and forced him to pick a direction and seek escape at all costs.

Helpless, he scrabbled and clawed until he was able to move upright. Then out of sheer desperation, he ran screaming and blubbering, aimless and breakneck into the dark. His face was hot with his internal anguish, streaming with tears that only terrified him further as they threatened to obscure his already poor vision in the night.

But that hate was even stronger. Hate was a sort of higher metaphysical energy. Hate, belonged to ssentient consciousness and required thought. And his nameless, wordless curses for this reality were more deeply rooted than mere hours of existence should have allowed for.

Long after, as panic slowly gave way to the rhythm of right human movement, he finally realized he was carrying something in his left hand, as its weight shifted fluidly with each pump of his arm, sloshing loudly back and forth within its container. He looked down as he ran, not daring to stop, and his eyes tracked it as it heaved back and forth in his grip, which was so tightly bound it was a miracle he hadn't simply crushed the thing entirely and spilled its precious contents to the sands to be lost forever. Even so, it was so badly squeezed, it barely resembled the clear plastic, store-bought water bottle it once had; not that he would have recognized it even if it hadn't been crushed by his balled fist.

Wrapped in some sort of tattered band with an image and bizarre rune-like shapes upon it, none of which did he recognize, the water bottle wore a label he couldn't fathom. In the moonlight and with his racing pace, it was difficult to make any sense of it, but the plastic shone like a talisman, so clean and beautiful in its seeming crystal-forged clarity. The water inside, mostly gone, flowed like magic light. Back and forth it thrashed within his grasp, promptly entrancing him.

For the first time, then, he took stock of what attached him to the bottle;

his own hand.

He didn't recognize it, but could feel it clutched tightly about the bottle so fiercely his knuckles ran white. He studied his dirtied fingers as best he was able while still running breakneck through the endless dark, and was equally mesmerized.

So thoroughly distracted by the bottle, its water's movement, and subsequently his own miraculous appendage, he didn't notice anything amiss until his next footfall fell further than it should have. He tripped, pitching forward, and his next step, along with his flailing arms failed to fall on anything at all.

*"Shiiit!"* He cried out a fearful curse, and for the barest instant something clicked in his primitive mind. Some recollection of what he was, or had been, came back to him. Not enough to formulate a coherent vision or even bring voice to it, but it was there, giving him a moment's elation and hope as he hovered in the ether between land and sky, suspended betwixt terror and enlightenment. He seemed to be floating for that instant, and he promptly attributed it to the talisman and the divine knowledge it had given him to use his voice in such a strange, organized fashion.

The word had come to him without thought. To him, the word simply was and always had been. It was some kind of power, and it uplifted him even as physics dragged him in the opposite direction.

He'd run straight off the steep side of his dune without seeing it coming. Down the side of it he abruptly tumbled, and all elation became a stunned new form of terror in what unexpected new horror he found himself in as gravity promptly came back into his world, master over him as it had been when he'd first awakened yesterday. It returned and took over without compassion. Almost cruel, it pulled him down with a sucking sensation in his belly.

He was not lost in an airborne ungrounded new world of flight. He was not magical at all. He didn't have time to consciously think on any of these attributes of his fresh, fearful existence, receiving only vague, swift, instinctive, sensational impressions from his five senses before he struck the side of the dune, and was cast into a prompt windmill tumble down its steep bank. If his running had been breakneck, this new series of furious impacts, too swift for him to truly register each, was sure to do what his running could not.

*"Shiiit!"* He cried again as the impacts battered him with shocking rapidity, but the dune was swift to take his voice from him, slamming his head, then twisting his body with the momentum and catapulting him into

the air, where he wheeled head over heels several times before coming back to earth again. The universe spun too rapidly for him to make any sense of anything at all. Several times he came to ground and lifted free again, and he was beaten badly by the glancing impacts. But he didn't have time to register pain until he at last struck down hard and came to a halt.

The impact knocked the wind from his lungs so fiercely he didn't think it would ever return. He coughed and sputtered and gasped and groaned and basically thought he was going to die, though he didn't have any right thought or term for such an end to things. But then a new agony rang out within him, screaming up from his right leg as if it had surely been ripped clean off.

He'd rolled all but immediately to a halt on flat earth again, he found when he righted himself, but he paid nothing else any mind as he wailed, clutching at his ankle.

"Ah! Ah! Ah!" He cried, rambling himself into a string of unintelligible curses from his previous, uncertain, forgotten life. So ingrained into him from his old life that they readily came out despite his lack of awareness of their existence, the words were little more than colorful, vulgar reflexes of an untrained mouth vibrant enough to make a sailor envious. Though, they were few enough to be impossible to consciously register as they came through his pain.

He coughed further and cursed betwixt rocking and writhing through a perpetual grimace as the pain slowly lessened and his breath returned. His head ached from being hammered against the dune, but even that, at length, dulled to a gentle throb. All the while, he sobbed and clutched at his wounded bits, laying curled in a fetal ball, and in so doing, he learned a small bit about his own shape, and a great bit about agony and injury. Instinct warned and screamed to his senses, gifting him the vague awareness of danger's many forms and the concept of maintaining safety for his person.

Eventually, he calmed enough to take note of how cold he felt. The desert air was frigid at night, and would have been frosty if not for its dryness. He shivered, and found himself clutching and hugging at himself with both hands in an effort to keep warm. It was just a new form of suffering and hell for him to fear. Reality was too much, a harsh and unforgiving, unfriendly state and place.

But even his new fear swelled to panic when he realized his hands, those miraculous appendages, were both working to do what little they could to warm him. Both of them.

His left one, particularly, was empty.

He'd dropped his magic talisman of crystalline fluid light.

He didn't know what it was. He didn't know it's significance. He just instinctively felt the weight of its importance. So precious a gem could not have been anything less than something he needed and wanted. It protected him from something, but he didn't fully understand what. Just as he didn't fully understand the threats of death, much less the many forms it could take. He certainly didn't comprehend the unreasonable fear the unseen reaper provoked within him, but he did feel it. It bore down on him like the eyes in the sky and the darkness alike. It filled him, like the pain in his leg and head. In fact, to him, they were all one and the same. There was no true distinction between pain and terror, hatred and sight, heat, cold, gravity or darkness nor self. It was all just a blur of being, and all of it indicated and led toward...not *being* anymore.

The swirling of the heavens, even, was but the clock spinning against him, though he did not yet register the concept of time either. He'd been awake only twice, and he remembered the first time vividly; all the light and the two colors, the oppressive heat and the terrible world of desolate sound and maddening screaming. They had all been too much, and he'd collapsed. And this time it was no different, but entirely incomparable; a darkness from the first moment he'd opened his eyes, until the moment he realized he'd lost his talisman.

At once, his eyes scrambled to find it, his one piece of security. It was the only thing he'd experienced in his brief time alive that did not terrify him - that and his own two hands. He managed to gain all fours like an animal, but the pain in his ankle intensified. He whimpered and clutched at his leg, but muscled through it, turning about rapidly as he searched for his bright, shining, sparkling, beautiful, precious thing. It took him a long time to look back and up the way he'd come, where he then spotted a glint of the talisman's shining light amid the chaotic track he'd torn in the dune-face with his wild tumbling.

The moon bounced off its surface like a diamond.

He gasped and scrambled up the shifting dune's steep slope to reclaim it. Hobbled by his injury, it took him some time, but finally he clutched the talisman. It crinkled loudly as plastic bottles tend to do when bent out of shape. The sound was sharp, but it soothed him, for he had back his precious thing. Then he hobbled and stumbled back down to the level earth, where he plopped down, physically beaten and exhausted and cold.

But his mind was still keen, and he sat there, staring into the bottle, admiring its shining and inner movement, and the way it felt in his hands; so cold. However, he barely registered the desert nights' crisp chill with that talisman in his shaking hands. He did bunch himself into a ball by instinct, warding against the chill, and there he lay, cradling the water bottle.

Nothing else in the universe had ever mattered before this moment. The bottle was now his everything.

With his mind not reeling in terror for once, his consciousness began to formulate coherent thoughts. Though, they weren't thoughts given to words, for he knew none. Instead, they were merely compulsive general conceptions about his very few known experiences, formulated more out of the very ideas he felt rather than the words that might describe them.

He studied the bottle with its tattered, strange paper wrapper, the indecipherable markings on its face, and most of all, the light of the heavens that reflected back out of it. It gave him courage, and for the first time, a vague sense of understanding of light and the environment of the world. He noted the similarity between the bottle and the sky, and tentatively lifted his gaze to the stars and moon and marveled at them. The bottle, whatever magic it was forged of, or wherever from it had come to him, was not only his; it had taken away the fear of the lights above.

*It had conquered them!*

These notions settled down within him, and he rested easier in possession of his gem, staring out into the darkness and its sky bugs, less afraid.

Some hours later, the world turned, and the sun began to lighten the horizon. For the man, it was subtle and slow, so much so, that he didn't notice it happening at first. Then he caught an awareness of the shift in color, and then the slow brightening of the horizon from end to end. It swelled and brightened until it was about to burst. The stars and moon slowly vanished and he felt as though he was sitting upon the precipice of a mountain he couldn't know, about to witness the most monumental event in all of the world's vast unknown history of monumental events.

The sun's body soon peeked over the horizon, and with a massive brilliance it shone. Unafraid, he stared, as it mesmerized him as well. For long minutes he was able to watch it emerge before it's intensity began to burn his retinas. When it forced him to squint against this strange, new, different kind of pain, he looked down to his bottle to ensure it would keep him safe. And sure enough, the plastic caught the image of the sun and portrayed the new colors of the dawning sky, and he felt as though the talisman had captured the rising thing in the distance too.

*It controlled them all! It contained them all!*

Dark and light, tiny stars, and pale moon, and now the first one he'd seen; the glaring one so bright it burned.

He faced it down, this new dawn, and feared much less.

And he came to realize the sun's great boon, for as it climbed and broke free of the dark line of the horizon, the world around him, a terrifying black shifting nightmare, became something he could see with a clarity not afforded by the previous dark hues and shadowed blues cast over him through the night. He noted and studied the lay of the sandscape ahead, and saw nothing that caused him fear. At once, he was emboldened, and totally relaxed with an audible and contented sigh.

At his back, the dune's lip had lit up like fire, and it slowly descended until he was staring the full sun in its blazing eye. But he was safe, and he knew it.

So long as he had his talisman, he was safe.

He yawned, a peculiar action driven by an even stranger sensation, but bolder now, he didn't even question it. In fact, it felt good to yawn, whatever it was to do so. He did it again, and laid back against the dune and promptly fell asleep; for the first time, at peace in rest.

\* \* \*

*He* awoke next, from dreamless slumber wrought of sheer exhaustion and stress, to the searing sensation of a full morning's baking beneath the desert sun. It was little past midday. The sun was behind the crown of his head, and he did not see it when his eyes slipped open calmly for the first time. He didn't think much of the sun's absence, though it had been there when he'd drifted off to sleep, for the scene was similar to when he'd last seen it. Little but the angle of the light and its temperature had changed.

At peace for the first time in resting, waking didn't startle him so badly as it had before, for now he had memory against which to compare his present.

He winced, however, feeling the tightness of his sunburned face, and the dull throb of his head. His lips were parched and cracked already, and his throat was dry and raw with both scratchy sand inhalation and the exertion of all his foolish, ignorant wailing. But worst of all of that pained him was the throbbing of his right leg. His ankle felt like a lead weight, yet fiery with pain. He groaned as he sat up, having slumped through his resting hours until he was mostly flat on his back, and he reached for his limb, feeling it pulse now that he was conscious again.

It was the first time he noticed part of himself was not the same as another. He was wearing denim jeans, but to him, his leg was blue and coarse, not at all pale and soft to the touch like his other appendages. And the very end of his lower appendage was like a blunt, featureless club. It didn't have digits like his hands did, though it did possess a worm-like and instinctively frightening mess on the top side; his shoelaces. It also couldn't feel when he reached down and touched it. His blue, denim skin also, was without sensation. Though he could clearly feel the pain beneath.

He experimentally and delicately peeled up his pant leg and saw a soft, white, hairy second skin beneath, which also bored its way under his hiking boot. His sock also concealed the familiar pale true skin of his body, similar to the texture of his hands. Its warmth there, however, was far greater.

His entire ankle and lower shin were swollen, and beginning to discolor to black and blue with his injury. The pain seemed to be radiating the heat he could feel on his skin. To him, these were also one and the same sensation. Heat was pain, and vice versa.

He winced as he poked and prodded at it, driven only by unfamiliar curiosity and familiar ignorance. Without even realizing it, he found himself reaching for his talisman, and clutching it to protect him from his wound.

Deep down, he knew for the first time, the true dangers of bodily injury, and he reflected on it as he whimpered and studied the talisman, pleading without words for it to take the pain away as it had taken away the fear.

But it was just a water bottle, and could do nothing of the sort.

Nonetheless, with it in his hand, mesmerizing him, he did feel marginally better about the sense of doom that crept into him when he looked at and felt how seriously his leg now hindered him. Like an animal, he had a momentary flash of the urge to rid himself of the offending limb, to gnaw at it until it was gone. But self-preservation was stronger and there was not yet need to chew himself free of an inescapable trap.

He found himself studying the bottle, helplessly drawn to what remained of its strange symbols. It dawned on him that it was damaged, like himself, and he felt as though it had done just as it did with the night and day lights and darkness.

It had mirrored them, and now mirrored him.

A caring wave washed through him, prompting him to delicately crinkle the bottle back into its right shape, or at least as close to it as he could manage.

Previously, he'd thought nothing of the talisman's natural state, and had automatically assumed it was complete, like himself, when he'd found it in his hand. But now, he felt like it had been around before his first awakening, his birth; not that he knew what a birth was, nor did he have concept of anything having come before. Not before this moment at any rate. Now, he conceived of something having come *before*. The talisman indicated it was so, and so, it awakened part of him enough to imagine it. Moreover, it signified that he too, was incomplete. That he too had a before.

Instinct formulated for him both the rough understanding that he was lost and that he was more than he was. But it also brought him the vague concept of time itself, the illusion of his reality given by his senses allowed for nothing less. Like all men and women before him, he was captured by it, and like most, conceived not a single explanation for it; much less a definition for any aspect of its finer workings.

He just knew *now*, there had been a *before*. There was this morning, last night, and the day before, in not so many words, and then beyond that, nothing; yet decidedly *something*. And, moreover, it worked in both directions. There was also, *after*. The concept of passing and time had both dawned on him so completely that his mind just readily accepted the notion without even the words to define them. The steady tick of his heartbeat even confirmed and cemented the concept itself. Rhythm and time, they simply *were.* Though for him, before and now and after, weren't what they might have been for a more educated person. He didn't have that realization. He simply knew that passing went on and seemed to have come from wherever it went.

There was no other explanation needed, and no other that would explain his talisman, whose strange runes he could never decipher. Looking on them with the new light of time, those runes were in fact, decidedly, incomplete. He confirmed it, as the label was ripped, and though he couldn't possibly understand them as he fingered the tatters delicately, he was sure they meant *something.*

This was the first time he came into contact with such a concept as *meaning.* It was the first step in a philosophical existence, like that which most human beings lived within, where everything was subjective or perceived as objective, and clearly divided by reason and logic betwixt the two, and, or could easily be misconstrued to hold meaning and *purpose* or in reverse, could be stripped thereof.

But now, that part of his human condition was awakened, and he sat there a long while, studying the label, trying to get it to show or tell him something; *anything* about this mystical concept of *before* - none of such concepts which he even had a right, literal word for.

When nothing availed and the sun began its descent behind the high dune at his back, casting him into the relief granted by the shade it afforded him, he turned his eyes back to his leg, his shoe, laces, sock, and finally his pants.

He fingered them inquisitively, studying again the difference between his various skins' sensations and textures, or the lack thereof and differing feelings of his clothing. It eventually dawned on him he was wearing a covering.

Just like the talisman.

He wore some kind of label.

He didn't call it that, however, as he knew not to call his coverings anything, though surely that was what they were in society beyond his complete ignorance. The label, he felt, was trying to tell him just what the talisman was. And thus, his own label was trying to tell him just what he was.

Thus, he realized he was wearing a t-shirt as well, his hands and eyes exploring the whiteness, strewn with large black runes he could not hope to recognize. Dirtied by sand and stained with what little sweat his dehydrated body had been able to afford in a vain effort to cool him against his sunbathing in the swelter of a sprawling desert country, it was just another reflection of his precious talisman.

He came instead to a realization of self that separated him from mere animals, but not by much. And he stripped off his shirt, fighting his own shape and mechanics in an effort to finally pull it up and off his head like some kind of second skin. Its presence disturbed him, so much so that he could barely stand to be within it. The time it took to remove, and the remarkable effort involved almost brought him to panic before he succeeded. But eventually, succeed he did.

He inspected it with a small measure of revulsion, noting nothing of any particular interest about it beyond its big markings, except he could now feel the cooling kiss of the still-hot desert shade. He felt less stifled without the t-shirt, and realized the other clothing must be capable of coming off as well.

Again, it took him some effort to figure out the mechanics of removing his jeans, but eventually he managed to decipher the button and zipper. In truth, they were so intuitively designed by ages of mankind's interest in clothing and styles that they almost did the work themselves. He had to but guide them.

Beneath, he had another second skin, a pair of boxer-briefs, plain and largely unmarked. He peeled them down as well and felt cooler than he had all day. It was glorious, no matter the amount of sand that got into his ass crack. Face to face with his own penis, he didn't even recognize it. He didn't even take note of it, so engrossed in his effort to unravel the mysteries of his garments.

He was almost nude when he came to a conundrum. His bulky feet coverings wouldn't let him get the leg skins off. He fought with trying to just tear them off for many long minutes before his advancing, problem-solving mind forced him to reassess the situation. It again took some time, but after reversing the pants enough to have clear view of his shoes and after failing to simply pry them off by force without undue pain to his injured leg, he managed to untie a lace quite by accident, as he was afraid to touch the snake-like, instinctually-frightening things.

Then, he managed the other in a more studious process, allowing him to pry off the shoes as they finally loosened.

His feet began to breath, feeling fresh and cooled by the breeze over his sweat-soaked socks. Those too came off, and he was stunned by what he saw.

His feet.

For the first time, he saw his feet, and he found himself grinning at the sensation they afforded him. He wiggled them in the air and buried them in the cooling sand and found the simple joy infants also quickly discover in their lowly appendages.

He unwittingly smiled like a dullard, laughed for the first time, and though the sound was strange, he was now familiar enough with the concept of *self* as to no longer be much puzzled by anything he personally emitted. He quickly embraced the laughter, and cackled wildly at his delight in nudity. But then he flailed too jubilantly, and his swollen ankle pained him, bringing him back from joy and into deeper study.

Side by side, it was easy, even for him in his infantile state, to see the difference between one leg and the other. Black and blue, his entire right ankle looked angry. Swollen and bruised, he could tell that he was damaged, and he made point to be careful with it, gingerly moving it when he needed to.

A new realization came to him then as he studied the differences between his injured and healthy legs. He glanced at his clothing in wonder, and his first rudimentary question came to him.

Although he didn't yet fathom the concept of questions, leastways not in specific, coherent, English words, he did have a *question*.

*What... am I?*

He found his body with both his eyes and hands and studied as much of it as he could perceive, fixing quickly on the strange appendage between his legs which he'd previously overlooked. It wasn't aesthetically appealing in any special way. Most of humanity agreed unanimously on that. But he felt it special, because it was part of himself. Moreover, some part of him sensed something of what it was for, though he couldn't put a finger on it exactly. It was something of importance, though. He could feel that much.

Then, he felt something else about it, or rather, within it. A tingle spread from it into the rest of him as he fiddled with it, and suddenly it was a fountain. He felt the relief of releasing urine, and sighed loudly and smiled all too proudly as it arced nearly straight up and fell back down, golden with his advanced dehydration, and splattering all over his own fool lap.

To others he would be a driveling idiot, a filthy bastard to be shunned as a homeless man who simply, unfairly, didn't have the luxury of a bath, but to him, so like a babe, it was a joyous, miraculous discovery and sensation of pure relief. And he laughed aloud, happy as he gained his feet and flailed it about without care to where it was flung until he was fully drained. He was so immersed within that small joy that he overcame the pain in his leg without a thought. Nor did he think anything wrong with his nudity, or his behavior, much less find himself filthy. He simply was, and he laughed until it was over, taking the same joy an infant son must feel blasting his poor parents in the face during changing time.

Then he felt he knew what *it* was for. And this fact of knowing something new, about himself, pleased him into ease.

He felt so relieved from the released pressure in his bladder that he grew tired. The ache of his injured leg also returned, so he thoughtlessly returned to his resting place and looked again at his clothing for a long time, eyeing them and all but distrusting them in these moments of self-discovery. He almost shunned them entirely, but then picked them up in deep study as he began to wonder about them.

*Were they his?*

Did he want them? Or had they been the source of his injury? Were they part of *where* he was, or *why* he was here? Had they come from the *before?* What did they say about him? His own label, should they remain? Should the talisman's covering be removed as well?

*Logic* swiftly swept into his reasoning mind, and he knew they were his, he did want them, and they had in fact come from the *before.*

He spent so much time sitting there in this process of gaining nudity and contemplating what he was and what all this clothing business was about that evening crept upon him and the color of the light changed as the sky began to darken beyond his account.

It was a familiar, blackening sky, filling with the little lights in the heavens that then graced him a sort of comfort in the concept of time's slow movement.

He recognized night and day, and felt less conflicted about his environment. But even so, the dark awakened in him a sense of exposure and fear, and promoted an urge to find shelter and protect himself from things he couldn't see. The natural fear of the dark crept back into him, though it was different this time.

Before it had simply been an abrupt moment when he'd awakened, and found his environment infinitely changed from what he'd first encountered, which would be startling for any man. This time, though he didn't have any sense of reference from the *before* to warrant a sense of danger in the dark, it was simply the instinct of hidden threats that rose up within him.

A chill swept over him, as the cold of the night began to creep into him, doubly frigid due to his increasingly sunburnt skin and unfortunate nudity. He hugged himself, but that was not enough. He rubbed himself instinctively, trying to get the warmth back, but this caused pain in his skin and still the heat evaded him. Eventually he turned to trying to cover himself with his clothes like blankets, but they offered him little protection from the penetrating cold.

In the growing dark he then spent many long minutes trying to figure out how to put his second skin back on. It had been hot when he'd worn them, and logic suggested he would be warm again with them back in their original places, as the elusive, yet-undefined *before* suggested they should be. He didn't manage to figure out his shoelaces, but with enough effort, he managed to clothe himself enough to take some of the chill out of the night air. Though, even that was little help against the desert.

The desert was like merciless, sucking gravity. It was a beast. It was a living thing, despite its desolation. It would try to kill him with the dark and its cold and its heat and its light.

Shivering and alone, he looked to his talisman for aid, clutching it to himself as he curled into a helpless ball in a desperate, futile effort to ward off the cold. He drifted off to sleep in the fetal position, unaware and unafraid of the greater dangers that would soon be presenting themselves in the forms of exposure, dehydration, and starvation.

Death. It would warn to any right mind, though not yet to this infant-man. Death was ever-present; a constant looming threat, inescapable. He'd already had a beginning that was entirely terror of death, really, from start to finish. And it had continued the second waking, and brought a handful of new scares, bodily injury becoming the most real of his fears of death's many fingers. And now it returned again with the dark and cold. But he hadn't yet fully conceived of life and death. Instinct alone had warned him to fear the dark and prodded him to protect himself in whatever ways he could against the unseen threats that might lie within.

But *why?*

He didn't yet understand the concept.

That revelation, and subsequent thought, would have to wait until the morrow.

* * *

**Through** his second night he had his first coherent dream. It wasn't lucid, and he did not understand that he was dreaming. He believed it was a new, shocking reality. He instinctively clutched at himself, seeking his comforting talisman, but it was nowhere upon his person. This instilled fear in him as he was confronted with an inconceivable series of impossible events, so different from what little he had thus far experienced.

Immersed within moving pictures of places and things he couldn't fathom or recall having ever experienced *before,* he experienced them as part of them. He saw mountains and trees, vaguely resembling the crude, stylized imagery on his talisman's tattered second skin, which he hadn't previously been able to identify as images at all. But more than this, he experienced them; their rich scents pungent and life-affirming. He felt rain on his skin, and both heard and visualized it pelting a window pane as he peered out its transparent shield with a grimace of displeasure on his face, as if he held distaste for a gloomy day; much as many people would do.

Though in his present state and with such fresh, untainted eyes, he found it all gloriously beautiful.

Of course, before this dream, he did not conceive of others like himself.

With this dream came a vision of *another.* Instantly, he had the sensation of *community.* Upon so simple a matter as merely witnessing another human figure, which he immediately recognized resembled his own in some general ways, a feeling of belonging swept over him. He was compelled to take in his surroundings, discovering a grand craftsman style home, something he couldn't fully fathom, but he felt completely at ease, right at home within it. It sheltered and warmed, protected and cradled him with its comfortable surround. He felt it was his, like his talisman. In fact, judging by the water on the windows, he felt as if he was inside his talisman, looking out at a world he didn't know.

The other human figure moved, drawing him away from his studies of the room and the world beyond the glass.

It was a woman, and though he didn't understand her existence in any way, the surprising revelation that he was not alone settled down within him. At that instant, his primal instinct was roused. It swept over all other sensations, and he knew the differences inherent between himself and this other figure's beautiful curves and subtle planes and angles, so opposite of his own. He felt a myriad of emotions and connections binding him to her. He felt protective and possessive, yet delicate and warm. He felt love. He felt and understood most readily though, passion and carnal desires, envisioning her breasts, touched upon by her long blonde locks, as they jiggled with her movement above him; upon him.

She was gorgeous, a beautiful thing with a seductress' figure, sultry lined lips, and a little upturned nose set below piercing and bright blue eyes. She became his world. He heard her voice. She spoke to him, nonsensical sounds as of yet, but for the first time, he conceived of organized speech.

Although her words were but gibberish to his fledgling senses, he could feel the sounds she emitted were structured and held meaning.

He longed then, to understand and know them, and a hunger for *knowledge* finally dawned on him. The desire to learn and grow became part of him, and once it took root it would never be dispelled.

But then the other was gone as the dream carried him elsewhere, somewhere dark and nondescript. He clutched for his talisman again as he longed to see and feel her again; for he was now aware that he was so completely alone.

He had so swiftly as that, acquired a drive, a sense of purpose, even if it was self-imposed. He would learn and grow, and he would seek her out. In the dark of his mind, he began to walk, then to run, scouring the void for any sign of her. The dark became the threatening sandscape of his first night awake within the desert, the sky riddled with stars and overseen by the mocking brightness of the moon. But the woman did not appear to him, and he found himself wary of taking another fall and injuring himself.

Recollection within the dream for the first time did not just span unimagined time and events he previously couldn't have concocted even in his dire madness. It also encompassed and made real the things he'd so recently endured.

Soon, the entire desert nightscape was an ever-shrinking place. The fearful imagined pitfalls awoke, grew larger, got closer, and closer, and even multiplied until he was backing himself into a tight circle of safe land as the world sank around him. This place of safety only continued to dwindle and there was no escape as the sucking sands eventually consumed it entirely, dragging his backpedaling feet down despite his desperate and frantic struggles. Just as he was about to be devoured by the earth, as though trapped in an hourglass, feet failing to put him back on a ledge and save him, he found himself awake, lain in the dark of the desert he'd just been walking, and curled into a pathetic ball to ward off the cold.

The transition was as smooth as it was jarring, seamless but starkly different, and panic threatened to overwhelm him. The memory of the sucking sands was strong in his mind, and he still feared the dream as reality. And yet, his eyes perceived such little difference between there and here, that for a time he felt himself still in those dreaming moments. He could not differentiate the two, as the dream was as real as he felt now. It was as though he'd blinked, and the terrifying events he was just enduring had stopped at his command. The desert had gone back to normal. He did not consider them to be separate, imagined versus waking reality. Like everything else thus far, they were the same time and the same place.

* * *

*Awake* only shortly before the dawn as he was, his skin frigid with the kiss of would-be frost and all but imperceptible morning dew that had settled upon him, it took him long moments to get his blood pumping, work out the cramps in his muscles, and ease the stiffness in his joints. He didn't yet understand how close he was to death's door, but he felt terrible.

His head swam and thumped. His body ached. Promptly he began retching, but successfully fought back against the urge to vomit effusively.

Of course, there was little to nothing left in his stomach by now to throw up much anyway, and he felt the gnawing of hunger hollowing out his bowels. He didn't recognize the sensation, or yet understand the need to feed, but instinct would pick up where his ignorance left off. He was hungry, and he felt the urge to devour anything he could get his hands on.

Unfortunately, there was nothing, anywhere, not for as far as his eyes could see.

As he warmed himself up, limbered his frozen appendages, and got his blood pumping well again, some new sensation graced him. He felt a stiffness in his pants, a product of his longing and erotic dreamscape. He didn't at first understand the connection, and he didn't understand the erection that caused the change that came over his trousers.

In his ignorance, he didn't pay it much mind until it became unavoidable. His slightest shift in position caused ripples of sensation to radiate from his loins. They were electric and pleasing, and he entertained them. He then exposed his penis and felt its aesthetic qualities had vastly improved. It had changed shape and size, and ignorantly, he sullied his own innocence.

Something primal came over him. He could feel it in his eyes, as if he had become a different creature, a different person, a different *thing*, where lack of terms failed him, and was then being driven by something else's thoughts. He enjoyed the touch of himself until it culminated in a body-rocking series of ecstatic sensations.

The dream of the woman was in his mind. She was atop him, sheathing him, filling him with that same pleasure, and he knew then he'd been right about the importance of his fountain. He knew now what it was really for.

Of course, when it flowed this time, it was an entirely different substance that emerged. But he didn't give it much thought, sprawled on his back in the sand, and panting his delight in wake of his climax.

He just laid there and lost himself in it until his heart slowed and the subtle lightening of the horizon caught his awareness.

He sat up to meet the sun, marveling at its recurrence. Like a lad, even both his miraculously pleasurable discovery of his fountain and what it had given him were easily passed up in favor of the next thing to come along. He didn't, nor could he, get hung up on any one thing as everything was new.

Now, with the return of dawn his speculation on the *before* and thus, the concept of time itself, were suddenly proven and more solid. He smiled in anticipation as the sun prepared to emerge, and he managed to gain his feet and think about what he had recently just experienced in the dark.

Both his dream and his masturbation were powerful things to experience for the first time whilst possessing an adult's powers of reasoning, and they awakened new things both sophisticated and primal within him.

The hunger for knowledge, and for the woman both dominated his thoughts; so much so that he could now actually think and reason on a level previously beyond him, though in no definitive language's terms. In wake of his blooming consciousness, and the endorphins released by his self-pleasure, both so amazing, even the ache in his ankle had dissipated all but entirely.

Though, when he made his first steps, its silent hiss reminded him of what had happened to him. As he looked on the horizon, he gingerly tested its motion and ability to hold his weight, and found it feeling marginally better. It had been iced, essentially, by the frigid night, and the swelling had gone down marginally. He could at least walk, and failing that, he could crawl if he had to. This pleased him, for his mind had settled on walking, not in any particular direction, until the sun had fully come into the sky, and drew him that way. He would walk that way in an effort to find the *other* like himself, but for no discernible reason other than that he happened to be looking that way and from there the sun's warmth and beauty began each morning. He didn't have to think about it. It was just assumed the sun arose in the same place every morning. After all, it looked like it came from the exact same place no matter where he was facing in a landscape that looked the same no matter where he looked. Thus, the first rule of navigation dawned on him, a primitive and rudimentary beginning to locating one's self in space.

And so, he walked east in search of the woman of his dreams. He would find her, learn from her the sounds and meanings she made, and he would be with her carnally. This triggered a vague thought as he remembered to pick up his talisman out of the sand and studied its markings.

They must mean something. He now knew the truth of that. They were sounds, but no matter how he looked and studied, turning the bottle this way and that, he didn't know where to begin trying to emit sounds that fit them.

They could be anything. He marveled at the concept of the writing of sounds that now settled over him, and once more thought on his own being.

*What am I?* He wondered, though certainly in not so many words, which were sounds with meanings he couldn't formulate to begin with, and certainly not coherent English.

*Where* am I? *Where* is she? *Where* are those great white hills and those green towers? *Where* is the water?

Suddenly, the talisman in his hand made some sense to him. His cracked, parched, sun-blistered lips ached, and his tongue and throat yearned for the water, just as he did for the knowledge and the woman.

Another reflection found there in his talisman.

Then he had a confusing, foreboding thought.

If he had been somewhere else *before,* then it made sense to reason.

*How* did I get here?

It chilled him to think of this, an ominous feeling creeping into him as he considered it for a long time, letting it linger at the forefront of thought until considering it without any answer finally frustrated him. There was a *before,* he knew, but he didn't have answers to this wordless question. He didn't have answers to any of his encompassing confusion.

He lifted the bottle to his face in the dawning light, the night still deeper in the sky at his back, slowly being cut away by his dune's descending golden light.

He turned the now semi-sensical bottle of water about in study, tipping it upside down, rotating it, then putting it back upright again, watching as the water sloshed around inside. Deciphering the obvious odd end with its white, twist-off plastic cap was the way to get out the magical fluid within, it still took him several minutes to figure out the cap couldn't be pried off. Eventually, he accidentally twisted his wrist as he gripped the lid in his fist, trying to pry it free, and just like that, he solved the riddle of how to get at the water.

He chortled a gleeful laugh, amazed, and unscrewed the cap entirely. He put it in his mouth, and drank for the first time, feeling its cold descend and flush through his empty, sand-parched throat, and then chilling his body down to his stomach. He greedily chugged the meager contents to the last drop, and banged on the bottle when there was nothing left. The thirst was overwhelming now that he'd given himself a taste. But no matter how he might try, there was only that much water, and no more. It was only comprised of so much, much like himself, and it hadn't been anywhere near full to begin with. In fact, it had been mostly empty, not full, which was also akin to his being.

Disappointed and unsatisfied, he glowered at his talisman, as much as he glowered at himself. It had failed him. For the first time, its reflection of his world and of himself had failed, despite its usual accuracy, and he cursed it bitterly. As he cursed it, he cursed himself for his ignorance. What he didn't know, the bottle didn't hold. He noted the dryness and emptiness within the plastic, as it mirrored the desert sands, devoid of fluids of any kind.

Empty, it also reflected the way his stomach felt. Now that the water was in his belly, he determined just how empty, just how hungry, he as. He could briefly feel his hollowed insides until the water warmed to his body temperature. He was empty physically, just like the bottle, just like his mind, and the talisman proved right again despite its momentarily perceived failure; a reflection of the world around him and of himself.

They were all one, he vaguely realized, feeling connected to the universe like some high philosopher gazing into the heavens, contemplating the endlessness of everything, the insignificance of his own person, and paradoxically, the eternity he was an inexorable part of.

He suddenly *wanted.* He wanted more. He wanted more water in his talisman. He wanted to be full like it once was, full of the world itself, and wanted to fill it in return. He wanted knowledge. He wanted other people. He wanted the woman and the pleasure she afforded his fountain. He wanted more of everything. But he wasn't going to find any of that here in this desolate expanse.

Dutifully, he put the cap back on the bottle, treating it like the precious and cherished thing it surely was, a miraculous container that held all the secrets of the reality that was him and beyond him and even *before.*

He put his eyes on the sun, and without a glance back, he started walking as best he was able, shoelaces flopping around in the sand as he went.

He would find the answers to everything.

\* \* \*

*The* hours wore on beneath his steps. The sun climbed free of the horizon, and tore its way high into the sky, blazing down upon him. The heat swelled and the land shimmered. He began to sweat out what little water he'd gained by downing less than half a bottle in little more than a few gulps, but he trudged onward steadily, ignoring everything but his desires to acquire more than he was and more than he had.

As he went, he thought, now fully capable of this phenomenon as never before. He only lacked the sounds that made words, or maybe just lacked the meanings of the words themselves, for as he walked, he babbled chaotically, half-delirious from exposure and starvation and thirst, and he tried to mimic what he'd heard from the other's beautiful lips before she'd disappeared.

He regarded the blinding ball of the sun for the first part of the day, burning his eyes as he walked straight into it until it climbed too high for that effort to continue.

What was it, that should make it so painful? It was so powerful it couldn't be stared at for more than a few moments at a time, but neither could he look away for long either; drawn to it like moth to flame. It didn't help that it was the only thing to fixate on in this endless expanse of nothingness.

Eventually, it climbed too high though, and he stopped paying attention to it for a time. Whatever it was, it was beyond his reach or understanding, except that it granted light and unbearable heat, allowing him to see the world he walked in and protecting him from the cold. Though, it was also a danger in itself.

This separation from the sun's distraction allowed him to think on other things. He started formulating vague postulations to answer his prior wordless questions.

The answer to the question of what he was came most readily.

He was a child of the world he lived in. He belonged here, and yet, not here. He belonged in that place of comfort, that home he'd seen in his dreams; a place with huge mountainous dunes painted white, and green towers of life; a place with water so abundant it fell from the skies.

He wasn't entirely wrong. He was a child of the world and the universe, though that wasn't necessarily what he was as a human. There was more to it he couldn't yet define. But he was close to understanding, especially when he recalled the vision of the woman, his mate. He didn't fully understand, as he didn't with basically everything just yet, but he sensed implicitly, that she

*35*

belonged to him. He was what she was, a beautiful creature with arms and legs and walked upright. He was something that had an expressive mind and a face to match it, though he couldn't rightly see his own. He tried, but it only resulted walking in tight circles with his neck twisted violently to both the right and the left and to no avail.

Upon that failure, he then really began to wonder just what his own face looked like. He touched it experimentally as he walked onward through the endlessly shifting sands, and found it course and rough with facial hair. His lips and skin, cracked and dry and blistered, gave him the vague impression of a self-image that was anything but beautiful by compare to what he'd seen in that other reality. That creature he'd seen was only somewhat like himself. She was decidedly better than himself in form, he proclaimed, and this made him feel the sensation that came along with understanding how lucky he was to have her. But it also made him pity himself with jealousy of her softness.

He was ugly by compare, his mind spat with disgust. He wasn't starting out in good place concerning his sense of self-awareness. But, he did have the thing between his legs which was special and gave him relief and amusement and pleasure. That thing all on its own tended to shatter self-doubt and pitiful self-image. He took heart in that occurrence, and managed to crack a painful, wistful smile as he trudged on. His one saving grace was his tool.

Though, he then felt even that, wasn't nearly enough. He was inferior. *She* was revered. But he did have confidence in himself because of it.

After noon rose and fell, the sun vanished to his vertical peripheral vision, and he came back from his musings enough to spot his shadow, cast on the ground ahead of his strides, leading his way. It was small at first, and amazing.

What was this new thing?

He tried to catch it at once, his eyes playing tricks on him in the heat with the dehydration and starvation setting in, but it was elusive. Even as he pounced on it, and buried his hands in it ravenously, he came up only with shaded sand. Then he realized it was like when he was sitting at the dune the day before, and how the shadow grew and cooled him. This made him think of the sun and its blazing heat. He couldn't see it anymore, and was left to casting about in an to attempt to locate it. Its searing touch made this a simple enough task, and he craned his neck up and back, tracking it high and slightly behind himself.

It blinded and burned him, somehow more intense than it had been before, and he began to feel faint. The world swam around him and he felt dreamy. He half expected to see the woman, for so familiar was that dreamlike sensation, but instead of her, he spotted something in the sky; a handful of dark, sharp, angular shapes, winging around in lazy circles. He fought to study them, but there was no piercing the glare of the hot ball in the sky, and their swirling started to make him feel like he was spinning.

He began to sway beneath the heat, and lost his balance.

For a moment, as he fell, he thought he was falling into the sky. Terror rose, but fell quickly again as he graced the hot sand with the back of his head. It seared. His exposed bits fried almost instantly, and he scrambled back to his knees, retching.

Nauseated, he felt foolish for his fall, and gave up trying to see through the sun. He picked himself up, paid it and its swirling shadows no more mind, and began to trudge onward again.

It was so unbearably hot.

He staggered numerous times but kept his feet, and promptly started prying the sweat-stained t-shirt off his back. It took him some effort, but he remembered how his second skin worked now, and soon he walked topless with shirt and talisman in one hand. His back lit up with pain, slowly frying through the march.

He was burning, but he didn't fully understand the dangers in that. He simply walked and walked and walked on.

His shadow began to grow a bit, and amid the swirling of his vision, he became aware of swift shadows swooping rings around himself at irregular intervals without any discernible pattern.

They had once been circling the sun, but now they came down to join the dark stain he cast across the sands. There were many of them, it seemed, and they were faster even than his own shadow, so he didn't even try to catch them. Instead, he grew hypnotized by them over time, losing himself in simply watching them as he walked. He didn't fathom what they could be, but speculated that maybe he wasn't well. He felt dizzy and weak, and could barely keep his eyes open as they seemed to be mesmerizing him to sleep. Perhaps they were part of himself, he even wondered, as though his own shadow had taken on a life of its own and broken free of him.

His strides began to stagger and stumbled frequently, and grew slow in his exhaustion. He was little aware of the sands descending beneath his feet when he simply blacked out. The light had stretched his shadow so far ahead he felt momentarily like a god, growing bigger and bigger, but it was simply a delusion. When, finally, the land went dark and all the shadows vanished into the black, becoming one with it, he fell flat on his face and was asleep.

* * *

*He* slept deep, body weak with starvation and dehydration, exposure and exertion, until he was fully immobilized by this committee's naturally-imposed law of exhaustion. He dreamt little and incoherently this night, the images coming and going in fits that made no sense of themselves, which made for a disturbing new reality to experience.

The temperature dropped predictably, but he didn't feel.

He was too removed from consciousness for that.

He was dying, though he didn't fully understand how. The thought hadn't even registered in his delirium. Maybe it never would. He might just die ignorant. That was a very real possibility when he was so completely unaware of the dangers he was in. He didn't even protect himself from the elements; not that he much could have even if he was more aware of just how many forms death could take.

Conversely, he might well discover the dangers in time and save himself, farfetched from possible as that might seem. It might well happen to him the very next morning, when he stumbled free of the chaotic indecipherable dreamscape of this night.

When his eyes opened again he felt the fever. It coursed through him, and full delirium had settled in. Exposure and hunger and thirst had already taken their toll.

His physical weakness terrified him. He did not feel like himself, or what little of himself he'd in short grown accustomed to. However, he did not cry out. He didn't thrash about, or scream his bloody murderous babbling terror as he had before. This time, he was too afraid and too feeble for any of that exertion or expression. This time, he couldn't even move, able to muster only panicked breaths that sucked up the fine sands into his breathing passages, drying him from the inside out as surely as the sun and air did from above and without.

He remained there a long moment, stunned by the return of the reality he'd been thrust into.

He began to experience *despair.*

*Where was he? Who was he? Where and who was she? How did he get here?*

These were all still unanswerable, wordless questions, as he'd already reasoned through them to himself. But there came then, a new one. Logic and hunger for knowledge demanded he confront it, though he still lacked the words to define the vague concept of the very specific question.

*Why* am I here? This new shot at problem solving, one of *reason* and *purpose*, filled him up even as his eyes leaked his meager tears of fear and frustration and very real sadness in his isolation. He was suffering, that much was obvious, and death threatened him, caring little for his pathetic state.

But *why?*

What force had put him here? What reason was there in any of this?

He silently cried, unable to bring himself to move under an already high sun. He didn't even suffer the racks of sobs. He just cried them out and panted through his driveling nose. His features contorted in agony, but that only caused his blistered face to hurt. That pain only spawned more tears of frustration.

At last, he felt the ever-presence of all-encompassing *death*, and it was only for despair's ugly head. He considered just lying there until this all passed into the *before* through the *after*, until he was somewhere else by the magic of blinking his eyes, but instinct and reason combined to tell him; if he laid there forever, he would never be free of it. In fact, it would come and claim him. He had to fight it. He had to flee it. He had to do as the talisman had done for him before, and conquer it.

Even so, he laid there, feeling the weight of everything pressing down on his back; or at least he thought it was just the weight of his silent sobs pressing down on him. That was to say, he didn't know the touch of anything but the sand and his own body and clothes, and could not define or distinguish a new sensation, such as a weight upon him, or the sharpness that dug into his sunburned backside as it sought to gain purchase. In fact, he'd awakened with that weight, and so, had no different sensation by which to measure it this day.

That was until that weight shifted and a sharp, angular shadow moved on the sands as if leaking right off his back to go stretching away before his eyes with the high sunrise at his back. Like a snake, it slithered and slid, and grew into an instinctively terrifying shape capped by a bulge and a hook that spoke even to his ignorance as a menace.

The real then came into sharp focus, cutting through his delirium and tears by instinct's forceful hand. He felt the pain and weight on his backside shift again as the shadow's owner sought to maintain its patient balance. It made a subtle sound as he drew a harsh, terrified breath to cease his blubbering. It was a sharp, cruel sound that matched the evil shape it's shadow suggested; a strange sort of muted, casual caw.

The vulture on his back dipped its head, and its shadow snaked across the ground toward him. Terrified, he couldn't bring himself to move. Then, out of nowhere, a second great bird swooped down into his line of sight, alighting in the sands not three feet away.

Like death itself, the vulture was a miraculous creature. It was however, hideous. Huge feathers on broad wings easily as wide as he was tall carried the beast to his deathbed, and its bald, savagely beaked head swiveled to take him in. Cold, dispassionate, starving eyes fixed him mercilessly.

Revulsion swelled within his belly, and he began to tremble with terror. The weight on his back shifted a third time as the dominant bird lifted its own wings at the newcomer. Its shadow changed shape to match, and before long he made the connection between shadow and beast ahead and the weight on his back.

He saw the talons of the newcomer, and connected them to the pain in his backside. His skin crawled, his terror became paramount, and he rebuked it all.

With a howl, he fought back, surging up where he hadn't the strength to so much as bring himself to move not moments before. He wheeled onto his backside, screaming his slavering fear, and lashing out with his hands like clubs. He caught the bird an unexpected blow, felt and heard the thump of his fist connecting with the creature's head and sharp beak, a fleshy knocking sort of sound like knuckles on a chamber door; hollow and cold and dull.

The poor vulture sought at once to both flee and attack, surprised to find him still possessing that much fight. It squawked and squealed, promptly deciding to seek escape in the face of his onslaught; for vultures weren't great combatants with living prey the size and strength of a man. They lacked the tools necessary for such opponents. They would battle against other predators, if there were enough of their own numbers upon a carrion find. They would fight their own kind for a stake at a meal, for food was ever-scarce in the deserts which they inhabited. But they were ill equipped to fight a man on his own terms.

He howled and grappled and punched at the beast, and something came over him. His killing nature swept in, conquering fear and weakness and injury where his talisman could not, and he became madness. He became the predator. It filled him with rage and bloodlust lain thick over the top of self-preservation. Driven initially by his revulsion, he found in himself the strength to fight and to kill. But then he lost himself to the greater instincts within battle.

The second bird flew off immediately, startled, squawking and terrified of him, but the first hadn't the chance to escape. He'd rolled atop it, and though it lashed out with thick dirty claws and fought to bite him with its wicked beak about his face, nearly taking his vulnerable eyes, he was beyond pain. If anything, the stinging cuts and nips only intensified his rage.

Fueled further by delirium, and then the swift raging of inexplicable hunger, he became the greater beast. He managed to subdue its dangerous beak by wringing its crooked, corded neck with his powerful hands, and kept its dangerous parts at bay while completely ignoring the furious beating of its now useless, ungainly wings.

Again and again he hammered the animal's tough neck and head into the packed sand, and it took a good many minutes of bashing it in this nature before the thing stopped fighting and went limp. Eventually, the man had broken the vulture's neck, and it only shivered and twitched according to discordant nervous signals. Then, it went quiet entirely.

Howling his triumph, vanquishing all fear, he found he couldn't stop. Rage and hunger still owned him, and savagely, gruesomely, he was soon ravaging the beast's throat with his teeth, growling and tearing at its feathers with his own claws. He rabidly tore the bloody thing limb from limb. He wrenched and pulled its flesh, twisted and snapped its bones, immersing himself savagely in the sickly wet popping and crunching of its ruin. He devoured some of it, feasting on its raw essence until he'd been drenched in its ichor.

His face, arms, shirt and pants alike were thoroughly stained with bloody streaks, some of it his own as the bird had scored a number of lacerations about his face and arms which he'd been too enthralled to much notice.

It was long before he calmed, and came back to his more innocent self.

And when he did, he felt terrified anew; not of the beast, or of the world, but of himself. He looked at his bloodied hands in awe and fear. They shook with adrenaline. Slowly, he recoiled into himself, and wondered at just what he had become in those moments of carnage.

Just what was he to begin with?

And again, he asked the wordless. *What am I?*

* * *

*There* wasn't much to be done about his physical appearances, though abashed by the act of murder, even be it in self-defense, he did try to wipe his hands clean of the blood and the life he'd taken.

He couldn't explain it, but he felt terrible.

Surely, the beast was trying to eat him. He didn't know how or why he came to that conclusion, it just came naturally. So he shouldn't have felt bad for beating it to the punch. He gained a measure of a sense of *justice* in this notion. But either way, he did feel poorer for what he'd done.

Something in the way that he'd lost control, and torn it limb from limb, gravely unsettled him. It wasn't that he'd done it, or even that he was capable of it. He'd previously felt like a god when his shadow had grown tremendous, so that sense of rights and supremacy over such a beast couldn't be the problem. He felt more a god now than he ever had. He was possessed of a certain power that nothing he'd yet encountered could overcome.

Rather, it was in the fact that here was this creature, something living, and he'd destroyed it. Worse, it was the only other living thing he'd encountered since he'd come into being. He hadn't previously conceived of other life forms. The only other he'd seen was the woman he was trying to find. He didn't question that it was alive. Logic made that leap for him. He didn't even begin to wonder at just how many different kinds of *others* there were. He just accepted that he was not alone, not only in his own likeness, but that now of others as well.

And due to that, he plainly, rightly, reviled that he'd taken a life.

He felt, sinful, though he yet lacked the words for it.

The *world* was not for even a god to ravage.

Others, even those who were different in every sense, were still others of life, and they didn't overtly deserve gruesome death or torture.

He had a sense then, a vague understanding of a new concept which connected readily with his prior judgment and lamenting misunderstanding of the world he was in, given the way his talisman reflected the world and himself, making one of all and all as one.

*Harmony.*

The notion filled him up. He ought not have done what he had. It wasn't his place. He had no right to destroy another thing. Yet the hunger in his belly was still there, and he was drawn to staring at the ruined bird and feeling that anguish. He couldn't help himself. While he hated what he'd done, and

43

rightly so, he couldn't stop the hunger.

However, if he hadn't killed the thing he might have learned from it, though he didn't readily reason through how that could have been accomplished.

He overlooked the fact that it may have been trying to kill him first as well, and despite the atrocity he felt he'd committed, he was sitting here in the morning sun, salivating at the taste of its copper. He licked his lips, and that hunger and bloodlust slowly came back over him again. He felt it like a living thing this time, creeping into the skin around his eyes. It changed him. It changed the way he saw, quite literally. As though some dark entity slipped into and became him, he could surely feel it, but he couldn't stop it. In fact, he reveled in it no matter how repulsed he was by the conceptual thought of murder.

He reached for his talisman in a futile effort to restrain himself and comfort his rattled state. But when he found it with his eyes, it too was streaked with the vulture's blood. It once more reflected his world, and himself, and told him all he ever needed to know.

It was this, or nothing.

Devour, or starve.

He learned of hunger in full, and the threat of failing to consume, and of death itself; and how they were all of them the same as him, the same as his talisman. Everything was one. He chided himself for having forgotten that, one of his earliest reasoning conceptions.

All was one. He was all. He was one. He was Death. And if he didn't feed, Death would become him, like the bird in his clutches. He wondered momentarily if he was now the vulture, but his figure hadn't changed, so for the time being, the thoughts of *why,* and *woe is me,* were put aside, and he succumbed to starvation and began to feed more thoroughly. The meat was concealed beneath the beast's prickly feathering and tough elastic skin, he knew, for he'd already consumed no small amount in his fury. All of it tasted metallic and plain, and the sheer motions of feeding were vile. He felt sickened by the cold mechanical act, and several times vomited dry heaves. But once he got through it, immersing himself in the meat and innards, it didn't bother him so much. In truth, the combination of both instinct to eat and so much hunger made the feast divine.

He fed and he relished it until he simply couldn't eat any more and felt he would burst. He thought the vague thought that he might be sick and vomit it all back up again, envisioning what that would be like, but each time his bowels threatened to expel the uncooked meat, he muscled them down to keep inside what precious life and red fluid he'd stolen.

When he was done, and had rested long beside the corpse in a daze wrought of his full belly and delirium, he finally found out his talisman again, seeking its comfort and reassurance. But for once, the talisman did not reflect him. It was still empty, and he...he was full.

He felt ashamed by this, enough so as to flee the scene of his crime against nature. He gained his feet and finally noticed the swirling shadows on the ground. There were several of them again, as they'd been before, and now he recognized them for what they were. Vultures high above were circling. But when he looked to the sun to find them out, of course it blinded him and he failed to much pick them out.

He felt so terribly about what he'd done, he just knew those shadows meant him harm. They were the same as the one he'd undone. They were one, just like he and the *other*. They'd want vengeance against him, as newfound vague *justice* predicated. And he considered that a moment, as it was an unusual thought. He soon solidified a stronger sense of the notion of *justice*, right and wrong.

*"I'm sorry."* He muttered unwittingly as he gathered his t-shirt and hurried away, an utterance so thoroughly ingrained in him from the mysterious, forgotten *before,* that he barely registered he'd said it, much less what it meant. But he caught it as it almost fled his mind, and he analyzed it as he fled the scene of his crime.

*I'm sorry!*

He understood it. He'd spoke! He'd used words! He was stunned, and he grinned, having forgotten even the guilt of murder and why he'd said these words, though he understood perfectly now what they'd meant.

For the first time, language itself, verily, English, had made a sliver of sense. He laughed and screamed the words again.

"I'm sorry!" He cried, and he repeated it numerous times as he walked on, headed in the direction the sun had long ago arisen from. He soon enough made a game of the words, and repeated them almost like a song, line after line after line, never changing, always sorry for what he'd done.

It didn't matter that he was speaking them entirely out of context or that after so many repeated iterations they swiftly lost all meaning. It only mattered that he was speaking them at all.

"I'm sorry. I'm sorry. I'm sorry." And on it went ad infinitum.

The vision of the woman came to him in his mind's eye, and he thought he was now very much on his way to acquiring her with his newfound knowledge. This pleased him. With a full belly of meat and bloody juices, he also began to come back down from delirium, though sooner or later, thirst and heat and exposure would catch back up to him.

That didn't matter for the time being though, for he could speak, he could kill, he could remember, he could walk, and he could feel.

For now, that was enough to keep him going on until night. So that's exactly what he did, never-minding the withering, scalding, ever-shimmering heat which grew strongest as the sun crested, descended and began to create lakes of light where there were none.

\* \* \*

**Soon** enough he was tricked by the mirages. He crested a new dune and stumbled down it amid things he'd as of yet never seen before, except for their healthier cousins in his dreamscapes.

Sun blasted, gnarled lengths of twisted and stunted deadened trees hemmed him, guiding him past a large, odd, pale rock jutting out of the sand off to his right. The sand itself flattened and became a sprawling bed of cracked, packed dirt so fine it had hardened to a sort of clay. A right man would see it for what it was; a long dead spring-bed whose water was gone, evaporated by the dire sun. But this man saw through heat-soaked eyes, and his thirst was enveloping. He saw only the lake that may have once been.

The shimmering heat-warped light bent his mind to its will, and deceived, he ran joyous, leaping and lunging into the chill waters, kicking and splashing up a spray. It dazzled his senses, and called back from the void of his lost memories, all the sensory experiences required to complete the illusion in full.

He frolicked at his salvation as even his new world's sense of danger and death faded away, leaving him kicking and splashing, laughing and dancing like a child.

With a blink, he was lost within memories he didn't know he'd had.

He was a boy, no more than ten or twelve, unabashed as he played in the shallows of a lake he remembered as clear as day. There were few trees surrounding, and only in patches, for this lake lay in a plain. Only undulating grassy hills were much seen framing the water's lay, largely dotted by wily brush, and the sun was hot in summer's heights, lighting up the murky water's surface with diamonds and glare and rays that only penetrated the dirty depths enough to see his calves descending into the greenish gloom.

He experienced it, immersed within it fully, and didn't care to contradict his newfound existence in any way until that glare began to hypnotize him. Then, he stood rigid and stared into its depths, blinding himself as the sensation that something was direly wrong came to grip him. He attempted to reason through the feeling, but as the boy he was stood dazed, scanning the surrounding lands and nearly endless expanse of fresh lake-water, he couldn't overcome the sensation of trouble.

He recalled the desert and the vulture and all that suffering he'd experienced so recently, and the mirage began to lose its hold.

Thigh deep in a lake, feeling its cooling, hydrating graces, he remembered something about that place. The boyish memories were filled with a sense of understanding which the adult infantile man couldn't fully comprehend.

The lake wasn't natural. It wasn't a problem that it wasn't really there in the present. That hadn't catapulted him back into the real, and dragged the waters back into but the recesses of his memory. It was the fact that the lake was only a reservoir. It had been manmade. Someone he couldn't envision had told him it was so.

He didn't understand such a concept, not fully. It was staggering to imagine, really; such a vast sprawl of blessed water being placed there by man was hard to believe. But, he felt the truth of it, and when he blinked to study the water with new understanding, there was nothing beneath him but the dry death of a spring that had once been.

The lake, being unreal in its artificiality, kicked him free of the illusion.

It stunned him with its abrupt end, but he found he could relive this memory at will. He easily immersed himself in it again, and the vision was so complete he could hear the laughter and voices of others, and he knew at once he was looking at the *before*. But he could also now differentiate between the two, memory and present. It had taken their overlapping in a conscious state not prompted by dreams to shake that sense of recognition from him fully.

Hungry for knowing, he fought to maintain it, to scrape the cracked lakebed and dredge the depths of the memory for more details, but the memory, as is often the case with those from childhood, was vague and incomplete. It was just a flash of a happier time, and despite its detail, it could not overwhelm his conscious eyes and senses any longer. It was only a vision in so far as the inside of his head.

Mostly, when he tried, all he remembered was the airy, humid and hot plains surrounding the child's refreshing lake and the joy of his time spent there. It felt as if it was endless, a span of time that was so lazy and carefree and fun that it just went on and on. Though without question, it had ended, for it was already gone.

Although abstracting the finer details of expanding on his little memory were lost to him, and nothing changed no matter how long he perpetuated it in his mind's eye, it gave him something that he didn't much have before.

It gave him some more knowledge of the *before,* a bit more of a sense of self, and just how far back the before could go. It went some long ways further than what he had even previously conceived as possible.

And just like that, he began to get other flashes of memory, none of it seemingly related, but for the fact that they were all his own memories.

He then stood incapacitated by the overwhelming rush of images.

He saw himself in a place where he'd *worked?* He saw himself in places where he'd eaten without the guilt of murder, and with *others* that he'd known; some quite well, others less so. He heard them speak, and felt his own tongue and throat working out the sounds of communication.

*Words*, they suddenly took on new meaning, new shapes and images abstracted from *meaning*, all of which only blurred together and confused him the moment he began to come to grips with them, leaving him further confused as to their meanings even as he extrapolated their purposes and followed their tales amid clinking glasses, rapid, repeated drinks and laughter abounding through the caverns of his empty mind.

Those echoes careened through his inner spaces, and rebounded off other memories, lighting them up like electric lights, which in themselves he also saw and divined as real, existing things. So unlike the stars and sun and moon, these things buzzed and flickered almost imperceptibly with their power. They radiated a distortion to his senses which most people completely overlooked, setting him reeling all over again.

Soon, it was all too much stimulation, and he collapsed to hands and knees on the dry lake bed. The dirt puffed at his contact, feeling hot and rough beneath his fingers, the cracked edges hard yet brittle beneath his weight. There the visions stopped all of their own accord.

Dazed, he tried to recall them again, but they'd been so vague and rapid, he could not collect them clearly. They spun out of his grasp like the sands even as he sought to put them back together again.

"What on earth?" He gasped softly, and he was surprised that he knew the words. Unlike the melody of *"I'm sorry"* which he'd nonsensically repeated ad nauseam until they lost all meaning as pertaining to why he'd first uttered them, these new words suddenly made sense. He knew what *earth* meant. He even knew alternate words for the same: abstractly envisioning synonyms; *terra, dirt,* and *soil,* all in an instant. He also knew the figure of speech he'd spoken and why it was used; an expression of confusion, bewilderment and sometimes disbelief. He was reminded then of what *I'm sorry* really meant, and its weight in relation to the vulture was not lost on him in exchange for the joy of simply having uttered them.

He had new words for that joy now.

He steadied himself and tried harder to think about what he'd seen.

He remembered the drinking. The alcohol. Oh yes, he knew what it was and what it did to a man. He'd felt the fuzzy happiness it wrought as he remembered his revelry, though he couldn't place any of the faces in his vision, and he couldn't put his finger on why or what they had been celebrating. But they had been rejoicing for some reason or another.

Friendship, comradery, communion, perhaps? To him in this day, those would have been great reasons all on their own to celebrate. Togetherness was a wonderful thing to one so alone.

Somehow that didn't fit, though.

Was it some event that had taken place?

It didn't matter what it had been about. Those people had been his friends, he realized, and he suddenly knew just how many *others* there were in the world.

A new vision came abrupt and wracked him. He saw, from on high, a city; great steel and glass buildings stretching away below him. And throughout, he saw the people, hundreds, no, thousands of them, all going about their ways, walking, driving, riding bicycles.

Others were everywhere.

The world, the Earth, as he'd once called it, was literally over-full with *others!* In fact, there were too many people, he sensed. Their machines and transportation, their trespasses, miraculous as they were; all were innumerable, and the noise of it wrought only unintelligible chaos within him, fraying his senses and driving him away. The revelation was staggering, and his senses reeled. But above all, his vision was most particularly overwhelming when it vanished like so many more grains of sand, and left him in his barren hell again.

He looked around in a daze, and wept dryly, his water-bottle crushed under the weight of his left hand. He was so alone. His world, like himself, and his talisman, was virtually empty. He was just so alone in a whole wide world filled with people.

How was that even possible? Where could they have all gone?

Some sense of sadness was triggered beyond the present at this notion's rearing head. He was alone no matter where he was in the world. No matter how many people surrounded him, he had been alone for a long time. He didn't know how he knew this. He just sensed it was so, and that was a terrible depressing thought.

Suddenly, however, to counter his sadness, he had a new understanding of *what* he was. He was a man. He was a person. He was...*human.*

The designation, however elating, somehow abruptly sickened him, and he couldn't explain why. However, before he could analyze the word, where his vocabulary was still quite limited, he came back to a prior, pertinent question.

*"Why am i here?"* He asked, driveling thick mucus out of his nose as he

sobbed.

*"Why am i here!?!"* He howled furiously, psyche cracked with vast fissures of ignorance. And he came to know anger and disgust with himself and his situation, and that triggered something still more within him.

The vision of the city and all those people. It came back fiercely, and disgust, not wonder, filled him full. Anger was its brother, and together they assailed and taunted him, refusing to give him any answer to his question.

He cried, cracking further under the weight of rising insanity, until he'd sobbed himself out, and his immediate feelings dwindled to yet again be replaced with his surroundings in the desolation of the present.

No new recollections came to him, though he pleaded of the void and nothingness for the answers he so desperately now desired, leaving him only with a renewed determination to gain knowledge.

Before, it had been a joy, a happier beacon and goal. But now, that hunger didn't even relate to the beautiful woman whom he would previously have himself primitively claim when he acquired the knowledge of speech and the means to take her. Now, instead, knowledge and his hunger for it was only bittersweet and self-fulfilling for its own hidden devices.

He'd all but forgotten about the woman, or at least regarded her differently from the caveman's savage lust he'd previously affixed upon her mantle. And that shift in regard for her promptly put her out of mind, diminished in some ways, and yet lifted to a still higher pedestal of greater importance enough to overcome his baser urges.

A dawning of *respect* for her was what had settled upon him, and having earned that higher state within him, she was then more easily set aside as secondary to other higher thoughts.

Overall, the visions, though painful in many ways, were also a boon that uplifted. He'd acquired some knowledge of words and speech, and could use what little he knew. However, he hadn't learned enough. And that hole threatened to defeat him even as it rekindled and gave a new shape to his sense of purpose. It gave him a semblance of an ultimately metaphysical destination and growth.

A new question then arose out of that fact, followed swiftly by others.

When he reached that destination, either physically or metaphorically through the acquisition of knowledge, would he be satisfied?

Would knowledge ever be enough on its own?

Would the answer to why he was here put him at ease?

Would understanding his memories of revelry and celebration be a source of rest, or just lead to more questions?

Would any of this ever end?

And... *Why,* oh *why*, was he even here?!

Knowledge, he realized its existence for what it was, was like a living thing, a virus, a double-edged sword. It would be a blessing to learn more, and it would change him indefinitely with every shred he acquired. Yet it might well damn and curse him further into this hell he wandered.

"Why am I here?" He asked again, aloud, trembling and unable to quite shake the sorrow that was filling him, replacing not necessarily the bitterness, but surely the anger.

Ultimately, there was no answer to be found by crawling along a dead lake-bed with its skeletal serpentine corpses of what should have been trees.

Ultimately, the answer was out there beyond this place.

Ultimately, the answers came from the *before.*

He had to get back there, and to do that he had to go into the *after.*

Struggling to right himself, and dragging up his crinkling water-bottle, he suddenly remembered it's label.

His talisman. It had writing on it, and he now knew the pictures of sounds called, letters, or at least he understood them in part.

Gaining his feet, his eyes eagerly scanned it as he turned it delicately in his hands, seeking something, anything of meaning in its tattered clothing.

"*Mountain.*" He mouthed the word all but silently. He knew the image of the mountain on the label for what it was, though it was just a highly stylized graphic. He'd seen the giant white capped dunes in his dreamscape, and now he knew their names.

He scanned the runes, not quite recalling that he'd previously reasoned the label to be incomplete where many of the letters were missing in its tattered state. He didn't recall enough of the language to fully grasp that there was more to it, much less that the spacing and capitalization were shredded akimbo.

And so, he simply read: *ure Sp i  t*

The talisman was called a *bottle.* He remembered that. A small measure of the magic and power within its existence sadly faded as he saw it with new eyes. But, the bottle maintained much of its importance, as it was his, and the water inside had been his. It also stood to reason that the letters may have been put there by himself. He didn't recall drawing the professional looking stylized mountain, or writing the letters, but he didn't remember a lot of things. He easily could have created it and failed to recall doing so.

His mind immediately connected the spaced letters even where many of them were missing. He fought to sound them out, but even broken apart as they were, he managed to make the sounds.

What had once read as plainly as day to any child as "Pure Spring Water," and could still likely be abstracted to the same by a reasoning and educated mind, even with its remaining letters only spelling out a broken "ure Sp i   t"

But it came to him only as...

*"Yuh, yooou, er...you're. You're! Sssp...it, it. Your sp, it. You're. You're spit."*

*"You're spit!"* he finally settled on it.

All of his sadness and loneliness and anger and disgust vanished with the rapid evolution of his mind. His lips trembled with pride and joy, as though a father watching his son execute the most noble and heartwarming gesture imaginable. And he smiled and laughed so proudly and so happy to have taken another step forward.

Just as with everything else he'd been through, he bounced back swiftly, like a child, and moved on. He didn't quite forget what came before, for surely he remembered it. He didn't forget his recent depression, or anger, nor any of the bitterness. But he let it pass nonetheless without suffering too badly a scar. The nature of man in his primitive mind; he was selfish and cared only largely for the moment. Past and present and imaginings of the future affected the mind, but only when one became sentimentally invested and focused on it in a present moment. He was not yet capable of such investment. Not fully. And his focus still wandered in his mind's inexperience. Thus, he slipped easily free of any higher, thoughtful, emotional entanglement.

He was not his old conscientious self.

Adam Penhale, as he'd been known by many before, was long gone and still unknown to him.

In his stead was a new man, a child growing into himself without influence, changed, even should he one day reclaim all that he had once been. And his newest discovery was a wellspring of such hope that it was impossible not to be selfish, seeking immediate gratification, and to feel elated and joyous again, as he had when he was young and splashing around in a lake.

*"You're spit!"* he shouted again and laughed, when his joy and pride overflowed. His mood swung completely reverse, which if he'd been watching himself, he might have identified as delirium.

*"I'm you're spit!"* he presumed the label, as his, designated his name.

Though he couldn't have been further from right if he was a left-handed step child of himself, he did feel it was right at the time, and so he named himself and repeated it without end.

*"You're spit!"* he cheered himself, and failed to realize the actual meaning of what he so proudly shouted. It didn't matter. He had an identity now. He had realized a semblance of true *self.* It didn't matter if he'd given himself the name or if it was even correct.

He did, however, off-handedly consider himself being incorrect a possibility, but then decided he liked the sound of *You're Spit* so much, just because he'd deciphered it all on his own, that it had to be correct. He would keep it even if he discovered his name was something else.

He shook his head. He wasn't someone else. There was no need to question it.

He was *You're Spit,* and that was that.

But where did You're Spit come from, and how and why had he come to be here in this desolate place of death and suffering?

Those questions hammered back into his reality, still lingering over his head, and threatening to plunge him into sorrow again.

He fought off the feeling of complete desolation, but those questions? They did sober him considerably, though they didn't get him so down as they had minutes ago. Instead, they grounded him, and gave him that sense of purpose renewed.

He would find out. He just had to keep walking.

He looked around, but couldn't quite recognize his surroundings. He almost panicked, but then saw his tracks descending into the dried lakebed, coming between the sticky, gnarled trees and to the right of the big white rock.

He resolutely pointed himself in the opposite direction as the evening settled in and the chill began. The horizon was growing dark ahead of him. It sent a chill up his back that was not related to the elements, but rather the fear of the dark, come to rear its head again. He clutched his talisman close to his chest with both hands, but it was not enough. Not after gaining a name, and certainly not after his battle with the vulture and his having killed something that wanted to kill him too. He now had too much to lose to risk his life any longer, or allow anyone or anything to come and try to take it away.

He'd evolved in instinct itself. It told him now, he needed more. He needed a weapon, and it caused a spark of bitterness in him. That word, that designation; *Weapon.* It sickened him just as much as killing had done to him. But he knew it was also a necessity. He had to protect himself, from the dark, and from beasts, and sometimes, he felt instinctively, from *others.*

Before moving on, he went back to the trees and worked at trying to pry free a twisted limb. He picked the straightest, thickest one he could break, and put his full weight on it until it snapped like a brittle twig with a jarring crack that resonated in the lakebed and shivered in his bones. He dropped the limb and seethed, wincing at the pain in his hands, but when that subsided, his work had produced a spear, sharped as a shard at its one end.

He hefted it, finding it very light for its size, dried literally to the skeletal bone it appeared to be. He swung it back and forth and nodded, satisfied at its whooshing sound. Then, he still felt he needed more. He didn't just need a weapon. He needed shelter, like that place in his dreams with the water on the invisible window pane.

But there was no shelter here. No matter where he turned, there was nowhere to hide from the coming night.

He would find shelter too, just as he would find out the answers to his questions, and he turned toward the growing dark, walking onward into the night.

In his rapid evolution here and swift vacating of this lakebed, he completely forgot his t-shirt bore runes to be deciphered with his newfound knowledge. And so, for the time being, they went ignored.

\* \* \*

**When** the night settled down heavy over the endless sea of sand, and the light had all but vanished at his back, a peculiar sound rose up that made his blood curdle. So unfamiliar with sound as a whole as he was at large, this new and unexpected call caused every hair upon his body to stand on end in a prickling wave of sensation similar to his skin's response to the encroaching chill of the night.

A wailing howl, it erupted at the rising of the fullest moon he'd yet seen, and though it sounded far, far away, it nonetheless roused his instincts and instilled fear within him. Weak, yet powerful, the lamenting howl crooned at him like a taunt, startling him into a swift panic. He scrambled into a defensive position as adrenaline abruptly flooded his system, and he scrabbled backwards, turning this way and that, going much of nowhere fast.

He'd heard so little of anything but the wind, his own blubbering and nonsensical words, and the squawking of the vultures since his inception that being several hours deep into the stillness of the night, it rightly frightened him severely to hear anything at all. It was simply worse than it would have been under the prior parameters by which he gauged his environment, due to the eerie peculiarity of a howl.

Though the moon lit up his landscape quite brightly in its fullness, there was simply nothing to see. He couldn't discern where it came from or what had made it. By all accounts it could have come from the moon itself.

He did not mistake the threat it represented, however. Somehow, he felt he knew what it meant, and to whom it might belong. He couldn't quite put an image to it, much less a name, but it was a beast, an *other*, like the others before and in his dreams; another life-form, one which he didn't wish to meet. That much he knew as absolute and true.

He kept his talisman close, and extended his spear out, as if that would somehow give him warning of anything he could see coming from the undulating expanse of blue lit sand.

Worse than the sound, which faded swiftly, was the silence that followed it. It roused in him a sense of impending doom, a mounting tension that made his poor, deprived sweat glands kick into action again, and prompted him into flight. He wheeled, trying to pick out what direction he'd been heading, and finally found his tracks leading back the way he'd come.

Then the howling came again, closer now, followed by a chittering sort of yipping and yapping. Whatever it was, it was dangerous and it was getting closer. Worse, it emanated from whence he'd come. He fought to see, peering into the moonlit dark, but there was only the unending, unchanging dune-scape. He broke into a full cold sweat, feeling the chill of the night settle firmly down upon him. His breaths came harried, puffing whitely in the dark and obscuring his vision, forcing him to scramble and run away. He ran for a short while before fearing too greatly to continue to do so without looking back.

He skidded to a halt, wheeling about and again peering into the night.

Something out there shifted then, a shadow in the dark, and revulsion swept through him anew. Instantly, he turned and ran, twisting on his injured ankle. It had felt so much better he'd forgotten he'd hurt it, but now it screamed at him, reminding him to be careful running in the dark. Pitfalls could be anywhere if he wasn't watching where he was going. This time, however, he could see well enough to avoid any major ones.

So, he ran, or rather, hobbled along as swiftly as he could manage, his loose shoelaces flapping with every stride, his hiking boots clumping in the soft dryness of the sand.

It wasn't long before he was sweat-soaked with exertion and terror, and as his minuscule fluid reserves trickled down his back, he was provoked into a breakneck race by the sensation it induced. He ran on and on for what seemed like forever, barreling through a harrowing shapeless nightmare.

As he ran, the land seemed to grow darker, the night thicker, and the chill brought with it a growing wind that cut across his heading and blew the sands in visible waves, like veils of gossamer black velvet lifting free of the earth and illuminated atop by the moon.

It was a nightmare, and it only grew blacker by the minute. Something was changing in the world which he couldn't quite understand. But he could feel it and smell it in the air. It smelled damp, like wet earth. It reminded him of his talisman and his dream of shelter.

Worsening the experience, he could feel the unseen beast breathing down his neck. He could feel its claws tearing at his heels. It was agonizing, unbearable, a sensation that centered in his tailbone and radiated through his body in overwhelming waves.

It was sheer terror's touch.

Eventually however, exhaustion overcame him, and he staggered to a panicked halt, wheeling around and lashing out with his spear. It whooshed through the air, making a low whoop, but struck nothing. He staggered sideways, overcompensating for his follow-through, and fell to his knees. Fear doubled instantly, and he scrambled back to his feet and came to huffing rest. He puffed hot breath into the night, and scanned.

There was no beast. There was no other. There was only nothing. His breaths were loud, and they terrified him. He feared they'd give him away, but he'd exerted himself too greatly to stop huffing. He tried to gasp huge gulps of air into his lungs to stop himself from making that ragged sound, but failed repeatedly. Even managing to hold his breath for a few seconds at a time availed him nothing, for his heart thundered in his ears, making it difficult, if not impossible, to hear anything but his own bodily functions over the building winds in the night. And this only amplified his terror as he was deaf to the threats.

Then, finally, he'd slowed down enough that the pounding of his chest diminished at rest, and allowed him to hear something else, something that wasn't his own creation. It was a panting, like his own, but higher pitched and rapid with excitement.

That's when he saw it. A pair of gleaming dots against the shadow of the dunes in the distance and the blackness of the now star-less sky. The dark was now somehow so complete it was difficult to discern where the horizon lay. Sky and earth had become one. It was thereby impossible to miss the lights.

The only thing the darkness made somehow easier was allowing him to judge that these lights didn't seem so far away as the stars that had once gleamed in the heavens.

These lights were nearer, and much larger than the stars. He could see them move in unison. They descended, stopped, then vanished for a moment, only to reappear and hover there in the dark. Suddenly then, there were two more, and they were even closer. They performed like the first two, and together the four of them stopped.

After a moment, another pair appeared off to his left, and they approached much closer than the others. They came, along with the sound of a hungry panting he'd heard before. He'd heard it from himself when he'd devoured the vulture that had at the time heralded his own death. But he'd turned that table around. His wonder at the lights was then stilled and outweighed by his petrifying terror as he watched the nearest, newest lights slow down. They blinked, but they did not stop entirely. They continued to close the gap between he and they, and they were a menace enough that he shifted his spear to face them.

Sweat beaded on his brow as he tensed in revulsion.

At his movement, the lights stopped and blinked again. All he could hear was that heinous, murdering panting, as if it was his own, and the wind howled through the thick of his own heart and breath. It was as though the lights were his own hunger, his own demonic self. It was as though they were the thing that had come into him and come over him and made him a monster of devouring and rage. But he didn't understand how they could come to him now. He wasn't even hungry at the moment. And he didn't want to murder anything else. He wanted to resist that urge.

The lights lowered, and he heard their bearer sniffing. Then the growl erupted. It was low and testing, but it set his senses reeling. It wasn't his hunger or a demon entity come to take over him again. It was *another*. There were *others*, he knew, and he had already realized that they came in shapes and sizes different from himself and his kind. Whatever this was, it was beyond him. He couldn't even see it, much less face it. It's growl was otherworldly and supernatural and it brought a new, impenetrable blackness to the world with it.

He screamed in response, terrified beyond all other actions.

The lights lowered, reacting to his voice, and the growl was picked up by the other lights.

"Ohmygod!" He uttered in his panic, pleading for something unknown to save him. But all he had was his spear and his talisman, and no god, a thing which he hadn't yet conceptualized fully in any conventional or religious sense, would ever come to save him. His knuckles whitened beneath the sheer tension of his grip, but he would never see it.

Just when it seemed as though this standoff would last until he was driven fully mad by his own fear, a light flashed.

It was far far away, back the way he'd come, but blindingly brilliant. Jagged and streaking, it lit up his surrounding where the moon had at some point also abandoned him, and he saw many things, some of which he was not familiar with. Cacti and rocks and sticky shrubs dotted his surroundings. The landscape had been changed by the dark into something entirely new. Gone were the endless dunes devoid of all life.

He had travelled far, and was now somewhere different, though it still was a place sparse and sanded. Every bit of it, so alien and caught only in that singular flickering glimpse, was a thing to be feared. The light came and went in but a shifting flare, and it was gone before he had time to take much else in.

Nonetheless, he did witness the bearer of the lights, and the gleam in its eyes. It was a lowly beast, but not so small as for him to overcome fear. It was rangy and covered in dark and earthen colored fur.

Coyote, or Jackal. He didn't know which, but the abstraction of the name jumped up to his terrified mind as surely as his heart leapt into his throat.

"Ha!" he cried, lifting his spear in a thrust, not quite believing it would help him. It didn't. The animal did not back down. The blackness, quick to return, also steadfastly remained.

Moments later, the great light returned, and this time he saw it arc down out of the sky and vanish into the earth. Miles away and behind, it throbbed, lighting up the world.

It was god to him. He hadn't yet created such a thing for himself to obey within his mind, but its power and awe was unmistakable.

Short seconds later, the first thunderclap called across the land, a deep crackling power that he could feel roll through his body. It startled him terribly, but it also startled the beasts. He saw their figures shift and hunch, their lights swinging back the way he'd come.

He had his chance. He wheeled and bolted onward the way he'd been marching all this time. At once the howls went up behind him when the beasts realized he was fleeing again, and the second thunderbolt rolled over the earth much sooner and far more loudly than the first. It filled him with its power, shaking in his bones, and he powered forward by god's great grace.

This time however, the beasts really were fast upon his heels, not just imagined. He could hear them and feel them often trying to knock his clumsy booted feet out from under him. A nip here and there about his legs and flanks almost sent him tumbling, but he pressed on, driven by the whips of sheer terror as the lightning flared once more, illuminating the lay of the land ahead.

Off to his left a rock formation jutted up from a depression in the sand, its base capsizing a twisted old length of tree as if the tree had come first and the boulders were placed later without regard to what they squashed.

He veered toward the high ground offered by the sandstone formation without even thinking, and took a nip to his flanks that punctured his t-shirt and the love handle at his backside. Instantly he cried out at the painful searing of the piercing, and his feet refused to carry him forward. The animal clung to him and slowed him, planting its paws into the earth. It started jerking and ripping at him, growling for his demise. The pain was lancing and ragged, and he knew all too well what it meant. But adrenaline and instinct were powerful, flooding his system, and giving him strength to overcome the hurt.

The other two were on him in a second, snarling and yipping as he wheeled on the first, beating at it with his stick and throwing it free with a strong kick. Off balance as he was, the others dragged him down with ease.

The first one returned, and the trio proceeded to maul him, yipping, growling, snarling and screaming onward for the thrill of his demise.

But some instinct was in him, and he refused to die. He fought back with everything he had, punching and kicking, then screaming back as they did to him. He gained enough room and presence of wild mind to start swinging his long stick until he staggered back to his feet. He surged up from the tangled morass of fur and claws like a sinner climbing free of hell's black, over-full depths, demons still clinging to his flesh as they feasted in frenzy.

He'd taken a bite to his forehead, and he had felt the points of their teeth rattle off his hard skull. It was a nightmarish image up close and personal, the savage teeth of the wild hounds, but it only drove him harder. He fought his way free with hard swift swipes of his stick, and ran on even as his blood and sweat ran into his eyes, threatening to blind him. The jackals pursued him every step of the way, harrying him, fighting his momentum, trying to drag him back down that he might not get up again.

But You're Spit survived.

He gained the sandstone formation, scrambling atop it and whirling about with his sharp stick. He caught the first jackal right across its face and sent it tumbling off the stone with a yelp as the lightning flared again. He saw the spear-tip gouge a scar across the animal's face. A spurt of blood shot out, and on site, he became the ravenous beast he'd been once before. Just as it had been when the vulture had threatened to eat him alive, murder reared its vicious head, and took him over. In moments he found himself lost to the flow of rage, screaming and howling more fiercely than the beasts themselves.

Thunder rolled across his stand, rattling his chest, and he felt like a god as he beat them back. Time and again they surged atop the stone, seeking to dethrone him, but he jabbed one in the face with his sharp stick, and it ran off with a yelp. The last he whacked like a ballplayer, stepping into its momentum with a tremendous swing that swooshed and carried the animal clear off his perch. The dry spear thumped and cracked like high thunder with that blow, and snapped in half, its brittle structure sundered. However, it only became a shorter spear. It was much less threatening, but the animals had had enough. The fight slowed then, and the jackals hung back, more cautious of his weaponry.

Thunder and lightning continued their dance, taking turns scoring the world, their frequency increasing and their nearness making them out to be the gods they surely represented. His plea for salvation had come, and surely did he feel the cold sting of a raindrop. Then another struck him in the face, and soon they were beginning to grow numerous beyond count. Their size increased as well, and in no more than a minute, he stood victorious, huffing and puffing amid the beginnings of a torrent under the crackle of the sky.

The jackals looked agitated, and curiously fled not back the way they'd come, nor ahead, but to either side. In the flicker of the lightning, he watched their figures climb the new shapes of his landscape until they rose out of the depression and were gone.

\* \* \*

**With** the beasts' departure, his breaths slowed along with his heart, adrenaline abandoned him, and he felt exhaustion seep back into his muscles. He was bleeding from a series of new cuts and punctures and scrapes, these worse and more painful than he remembered feeling after his encounter with the vulture. These truly stung and burned and broke him down.

He slumped to wincing a seat atop his rocky ramp, hugging his legs and sobbing into his knees drawn up to his chest. The lightning and thunder cast their rains, washing him clean of the incident, but also bathing him in their icy desert chill. He soon began to shiver in tune with his shuddering cries.

How could anything get any worse, he could have wondered, if he could have formulated the words to put that feeling into a coherent thought to describe his despair.

But he had survived. His talisman had kept him going this long, and the spear had helped where the talisman had failed. With his water-bottle on his mind, he realized he didn't have it anymore, and he managed to sniffle back his tears and choke down his sobs long enough to search for it.

He'd dropped it during his struggle, and he needed it back. He didn't even consider the fact that he was engulfed in the downpour, an abundance of water the likes of which he hadn't yet seen any sign of since his dream some days ago. But he would realize it soon enough.

As he spotted his water bottle floating in a swiftly forming puddle, he recognized what godsend was occurring around him. He'd asked for salvation, and it had come; not only in the distraction of the lightning and thunder gods that afforded him a head start at escape, nor in the high ground that had appeared not a moment too soon to give him a pedestal to place himself upon for once, and from which to defend himself and his right to live, but in the rainwater itself with which he was being blessed. Salvation, he instinctively reasoned, when asked for, came in all forms at once.

One was all. All was one. All over again.

He swiftly stood up again and rushed down his defensive pinnacle. But he was fearful to leave his high ground until he scanned thoroughly to ensure the jackals had in fact moved on.

Once satisfied that he was in fact alone, a reality he'd previously mourned, he scurried to the puddle and retrieved his bottle. He hunkered down in the clean, but sediment-riddled puddle and hastily unscrewed his talisman's cap, immersing it enough to fill it. Of course, the puddle wasn't deep enough to get a full bottle out of it. Every time he tried, it inevitably spilled much of it by being tipped on its side. That was until the puddle began to grow. Soon, it was deeper than his wrists as he planted one hand on the muddy earth to support his effort. In moments, it was deeper still.

The downpour hammered on the land in sheets so thick he could see them even in the utter dark. Of course, the way the water fell and pelted upon him, running into his eyes, made seeing much more than this a difficult task indeed.

He began to sense the danger somehow. The water was deep enough to fill his bottle full, and he did, but when he stood up, it was already almost up to his knees. He hesitated, recalling his vision of being a boy in a lake, and for a long moment he was lost to that memory.

The lightning crashed right over his head, filling the sky with its iridescent net, and its instantaneous thunderclap report jarred him free of his waking dream. The water wasn't just deepening. It was moving, flowing, and quickly at that, pushing him toward his high pedestal. He obeyed its thrust, capped his bottle, and sloshed his way back to his high ground. Around it the water was already filling in, making an island of it. Despite his sense of danger, his high ground had been a safe haven before, and he trusted it. He hunkered down against the wet and cold and clutched his refilled talisman to his chest.

*So much water!* He marveled, opening his mouth to the sky to easily catch several full gulps of precious life.

Of course, he wasn't safe. Not in the least. He'd been saved from the jackals by a rock and the storm and the demon that came over him when it came time to kill, but they all then proved to be his undoing. He was not the biggest killer here.

A new rumble, a sort of roar, graced his ears over all the tumult that hammered down around him. It emanated from the direction from which he'd come.

He was in a depression in the land, and when the flash flood came, it devoured his high ground in a matter of moments. At first, it was a marvelous event, the dark rapids raging around his defensive stand, but it soon lapped its way up the stone until it was covering his feet.

Quickly then, fear began to settle in again. He ran out of safe high ground quite swiftly, the waters ravenously consuming the rock until he was standing within them. Then they deepened still further, a sucking cold blackness that began to break his footing and drag him down like the sands in his dreams.

It didn't take long for the water to succeed in that effort. Like a living thing, it tore him down, and cast him adrift. There was nothing he could do to stop it.

When it happened, it was swift and none-too-gentle. One moment he'd been fighting the growing depth and current, and the next, he was simply floating along in the waters, clutching to his little stick and his now heavy talisman. Of course, he didn't know how to swim. He didn't even know that was possible. So, he quickly went under and only came up on instinct, kicking and sputtering, coughing and flailing futilely all at once as the water filled his lungs and threatened to drown him in their dark depths.

He fought it with every ounce of panic in his being, but that only made matters worse. Soon, there was nothing to do but hold his breath and clutch his talisman to his chest with both hands as he curled into a ball and bobbed down the raging river's way. Soon, his breath gave out and he sank like the stone he surely physically resembled.

He blacked out, but as swiftly as the raging river had formed, it bounded down a series of carved steps in the desert earth and deposited him on a crudely formed rocky embankment, and there he lay unconscious as the rains passed and the impromptu waterway drained itself out into the land ahead.

He had no idea how far he'd been dragged, nor where he'd ended up, as he'd lost consciousness.

But he was not dead. Not yet.

He came to consciousness anew just moments after he should have died on that impromptu riverbank, coughing and sputtering up lungfuls of dirty water, only to collapse and black out again.

Saved by reflex alone, he plunged back into darkness once more, and there he was immersed in a new vision.

\* \* \*

*This* was a familiar vision, yet it was entirely new. The visuals were the same as some of his prior memories, but there came along with them a different sense of the space; both which he viewed and within himself.

He had an awakening, as some small piece of his identity came back to him in his subconscious state. It was monumental, not only to he with so little knowledge of self, but also in what significance it bore. It could quite literally be considered then, no small recollection at all, despite the tiny fraction of self it represented.

He was back on high in a city, looking down at the throngs of the masses. And much was the same as it was the first time he realized the true possible count of *others* in the world beyond his desolation. However, he experienced a shift within himself, and he saw the scene clearer with different eyes; eyes worn by a man aware of what he was doing there. More than this, he had a sense of purpose in the masses below; not in their daily routines and private business, for one could never make sense of the chaotic movements of mankind no matter how high his vantage. Rather, he had a sense that they were there for a reason.

And then it hit him as he looked down to see so many unfamiliar faces.

They were all of them, gazing back at him.

Gone was the chaos. Gone were all of their personal endeavors.

Instead he became aware that they were all of them, looking to him. Some gazed up at him with hope. Some with sadness. Other beseeched him for answers to unspoken questions. But all of them regarded him *for* something or other.

A great sense of duty and pride weighed upon him, heaped upon his shoulders. The burden bore him down, yet he felt as if he could flex it like a physical appendage. He felt as if he had wings sprouting from his back, and he flexed them, envisioning at once the concept of a divine angelic self. But that vision came and went, and was replaced by the image of the vulture. It hovered before him, looming over him, a grotesque creature of blackness, become him. It naturally manifested in him a sense of doom and failure and death despite having conquered the beast in the desert, which in itself now lay forgotten as if it never was. It made him a manifestation of these things as well.

It *was* death. He sensed it's inexorable intent. It stared at him, prodding him to sit still as he was, and do nothing but pursue his purpose with his stoic poise; forever patient as it stood there waiting for him to die that it might at long last claim him for his...foolishness?

A sense of shame swept over him, and he could not bear to look the beast in its black eyes any longer. He looked down again to the people, and they shed tears for him as his burden grew heavy and laid him down. Cross-legged, he bowed before the beast and bowed below his own sense of duty until darkness returned.

They were one and the same, he and death. One was all, and all was one. He sat and bowed abashed before himself and all that he was and all that he'd done.

But his vision did not end there.

He woke as soon as his forehead touched the floor, and sat bolt upright, still cross-legged as he occupied a makeshift dais. The construction was temporary, and set on a street-corner, a very famous and populous street corner, one which was immediately familiar to him, and likely familiar to many, many *others*.

He had a sense that time had shifted. But, somehow, he hadn't awakened later. He'd awakened *sooner*. Time, vague and enigmatic as it was for him, had rolled backwards somehow. But he quickly identified what he was looking at. Ever eager for knowledge of the *before*, he was pleased by seeing this moment before the last and come after the first. He eagerly scanned his surroundings, watching it all come sharply into focus.

Chaos reigned around him.

Times Square, New York, surrounded him. Streets and sidewalks alike, filled with vehicles and people going about their business. It was his vision from on high, only now from down low. He didn't know it was New York by name, for that recollection escaped him, but he knew this place. Not many didn't. Most had at least seen it in photographs, magazines, newspapers, or on television, a beating heart of traffic and lights and signs to his senses.

The chaos of it slowly faded as he came to grips with its familiarity until he could focus on his immediate surround. There were many people gathered around his dais, kept at bay by a temporary little galvanized fence set in place to keep him undisturbed like a god's holy white ribbon of safety.

The people stood and stared at him as they had when he was on high. More came, some went, and others merely passed by the congregation; though even they cast a long look at him as they crossed the streets on lined-out walks between traffic intervals.

So overjoyed just to be seeing *others* and in such numbers, he couldn't do anything but smile in awe. He dared not bring his voice out, for fear it would fail him in his inability to speak much of the language of words he had forgotten when he'd awakened in the desert. But the looks on the faces of the throng was a collective plea for his voice. They wished to hear what he would have to say. They wished for it desperately.

He started to speak, to open his mouth and attempt to formulate sounds into words, but he stopped before uttering so little as a squeak.

His mind was blank. He couldn't recall how to talk, and he was afraid to attempt it. He looked down, and saw himself dressed in his scripted white t-shirt and blue-jeans, bathed in sunlight streaming down through the towering buildings so that he sat in an island of light such that he seemed to glow.

He looked around in surprise. The white fence, his glow, the people pleading for his word. He couldn't explain where the connection came from, for he hadn't previously fully conceived of the notion of God, not even yet after the lightning had come at his plea for salvation. He had but only touched upon the notion in the existence of thunderbolts, the salvation they afforded, his talisman, his shadow, and his conception of the *all* and its relation to the *one*. But in that very moment, he felt like a god again.

He felt important, powerful, as he had when he'd been connected to his talisman and the heavens and the earth and all that his water-bottle reflected. He felt primal, enveloping, and dangerous as well, as he had when he'd slain the vulture of death and feasted on its flesh and fought back the Jackals. Guilt was also in him, but only so much of it, and it was easily outweighed by his own importance. In fact, his guilt, his sins, made him stronger. They made him mortal despite his godliness. They made him identifiable. They connected him to the throng of onlookers and made him human. And it was as equal a part of him as every other part.

He felt suddenly, as if everything was spinning. He felt out of control.

The light intensified, and the recollection of the vulture and all and the talisman and his desolation dragged him away from the vision in a flash of blinding intensity.

He reached for it, desperate to cling to the *others,* to *be* with them, and not fall back into the isolation he'd been made to endure. They reached out for him too, as if they could save him from his fall, but kept at bay by the distance between them, they reached to no avail. He felt a pull, as if those wings on his back, the very wings of death, had returned and were filled with a violent wind.

He opened his mouth in desperation against the pull. He felt only the need to express the sensation he was experiencing as the world beyond his immediate surroundings faded behind the flare of white, as if explaining his sensations was the most important knowledge he could impart to any of them; knowledge they were there to acquire from his ignorant lips. But when his frightened voice came out, all he could formulate was the nonsensical.

"You're Spit!" He imparted upon them, and with that utterance, the vision was destroyed by his recollection of the present.

It was simply, immediately, gone.

\* \* \*

My Brother's Destroyer
by Clayton Lindemuth

*The* morning sun split his eye.

He coughed and sputtered himself awake, unable to stop himself from coming back from his dreamscape.

The flash flood waters had already receded, the majority flowed onward, and the rest had been devoured by the hungry sands and thirsting plants and the brutal, broiling sun.

He laid upon a pebble-strewn sand bank, dotted sparsely with the vibrant colors of rapidly blooming yet pathetic looking plants, those ruined by the harsh climate yet sustained just enough to carry on in their wretched lives. They were a new experience in and of themselves for him, so bright, so beautiful, so different from everything he'd in short come to know of this world. At once, he noted they were similar to himself in their more dismal aspects. They were another reflection of the all, amazing, but he ached desperately from head to toe; he could not pay them the attention and study they might otherwise have garnered from his fresh mind.

Battered and bruised by the temporary river, clawed and pecked and bitten by the vulture and the jackals, still a little ginger in his ankle by his own foolish hand, and burned thoroughly by the withering sun, he and his clothing alike were in shambles. Starving despite his raw avian meal, and parched despite his drenching in the rains and his float down the river's raging as they'd overwhelmed him, he now shivered despite the heat.

Delirium had been traded for exposure's instigation of full illness. He'd caught something, and his body was hot, but at once freezing in the sun.

His thirst prompted him to seek his talisman, but his hands, he discovered, were empty. Panic swept into him again, a now familiar state for him, and all of his suffering was cast aside. He bolted upright, scanning his surroundings as he had in his dream.

His talisman. It was lost.

Frantic, he looked up and down the embankment, but no shining plastic called back to him. There were only the dark sands where the water had been deepest and the earth was still damp.

"No. No!" He muttered, then cried, and he scrambled to his feet, rushing down the river's soft basin in what he could only assume was the direction he'd been moving. He didn't stop to consider if he was walking into the sun as he had been, though he still was. He simply scoured for his connection to himself, the earth and the heavens, and even, the all itself. He needed his talisman more than anything. It was all that had gotten him through all that he'd endure thus far, and without it, he sensed, he would surely meet the vulture once again.

He didn't consider how that could be possible, since he'd slain it and conquered the death it represented. But he had a wild, childlike imagination where anything was possible, and the recurrence of death's ugly head was not at all inconceivable. In truth it was inevitable.

He had sensed it in his dream. The vision had showed him death, though death had been killed already. There was no mistaking its sort of supernatural power. It was beyond even its own power. It could not be defeated indefinitely. Unlike anything else in the all, it could not be killed.

It could return, and it would, if he didn't have his shield.

He needed that bottle.

Eventually, after many long minutes of scampering toward the rising sun, he rounded a sharp curve in the drying riverbed, stumbled through a stand of dwindling water, and dropped down off another little waterfall cliff of naturally hewn sandstone. And there not much further ahead, he spotted his beloved talisman.

It shone in the morning light, a gemstone that fixed his eyes and drew him as only god could do. It encompassed him and flooded him with a relief found only in absolution and salvation.

He rushed to it as it sat in the lee of a gnarled shrub of sage-brush, glinting from the dappling shadows. He nearly reached it, but fell over his own feet in the effort, and crawled the last few yards.

Just as he was about to reclaim it by hand, a harsh and deadly sound erupted from the bush, as if to forbid him what was rightfully his with an eerie burning warning.

It sounded like the rain. Yet, it sounded like a vibration, more ordered than the chaotic impact of precipitation. It was fast and shrill and high, a fiery whining sort of rattling that only his instincts warned was bad. The rattle was violent, and both it and his instincts came late. But they both rose soon enough to freeze him where he was and urge him to recoil.

But he could not recoil.

He knelt extended and terrified as he gazed into the now familiar eyes of death itself.

It had returned. It had come back to him. He felt it in his belly, a cold sensation, entirely opposite, but at once identical to that first cold drink of water he'd ever taken.

Death had come back, as he reasoned it would, and it had taken a new, more terrifying form.

It was smaller, less grotesque, but infinitely deadlier. Its body was bunched on the far side of the stunted sage bush, a mess of dark, diamond-patterned coils of pure muscle covered in jagged flecks of overlapping armor. Its head was a compact thing with full and puffy cheeks, bearing two great, unblinking eyes, seen for what they were by the brilliance of their yellow and the darkness of their razor-edged, vertical slits.

The rattlesnake's blackened, blue tongue abruptly flickered out, startling poor You're Spit.

He started, twitching of terror, but caught himself. He dared not move an inch, and certainly not suddenly. He didn't know how or why he knew this was death. It just felt the same. Its jagged looking features were much changed from when he'd last seen it, but there was no mistaking who he'd met once again.

Death was growing all too familiar to him now. He'd seen it in several different forms, and it wasn't likely to stop coming for him. But he'd bested it before, and a measure of confidence filled him.

Cautious, he slowly backed away and calmed himself. The serpent watched him, and rattled incessantly. But it did not relax at all, content to guard over his talisman, seethe its heinous sound, and lord it over him like a taunt. Soon, he was beyond the rattlesnake's reach, and it appeared to relax a bit. Of course, its rattle still did not cease, a steady buzz that filled the area with its harshness.

He calmed as he backed away begrudgingly until he considered himself basically safe. But his talisman called to him. Its bright glimmer beckoned him back. It was like him. It wanted to be with him just as much as he wanted to hold it again.

Recalling how he'd bested death before, most immediately by beating the jackals with a long spear, he quickly cast about for anything he could use as a weapon. There were no trees, just sparing little bushes, most of which were prickly, and some of which were simply cacti, neither of which had he yet come across, but for in the dark during his flight from the hounds. But the cacti were even sharper looking than the serpent, and impossible to wield as weaponry.

The only thing of any use that he could find were stones. Some were too big to be carried, and most were too small to do much harm to the big rattler. But there were a few that were just the right size for him to lift with some considerable effort, and maybe drop upon the snake. He imagined being able to contain the snake under the whole of one stone, and capture death forever.

But he immediately doubted it would work. It had come back from death before, and it had changed shape many times. It didn't even need its shape. Sometimes, he reminded himself, it didn't need anything. It could be invisible, like the cold, and threaten him with nothingness itself, as it had with gravity alone.

The best he could do was scare it away long enough to reclaim his talisman, and be away from this new place as fast as he could.

Lugging a stone back toward the rattlesnake's guard, his steps a series of alarming, lumbering vibrations in the sands, the beast quickly reinstated its fervent rattling, emitting such a buzz that it seemed to be echoing from several places at once.

He quickly became confused and frightened, imagining death had multiplied and surrounded him, lighting up every bush with its abrasive fiery sound. But the only way to end it was to proceed.

He got as close as he dared, and the rattlesnake swiveled swiftly to face him, a series of sharp jerking movements of its curved poise that brought it to fix him squarely. It wavered, shifting as if afraid of him, and both gauging his worth and daring him to come closer simultaneously. Its rattle intensified still, and he steeled himself for what would come next, dreading that moment when he felt the hunger and bloodlust slip into his eyes.

He didn't want that. He didn't want to be a killer. But he had to. This time, it was necessary again. Just once more. He paused, considering it, building up his courage and holding that heavy rock low before himself.

With the vulture, in wake of its gruesome death, he had felt badly, and he recalled what he had thought at that time. He might have done things differently then, and maybe communicated with the thing somehow, and learned from it. He considered that might be worth trying here.

He knew death after all. He knew this creature. Perhaps he might reason with it. But as soon as he thought of doing so, he realized he couldn't speak well, and having a conversation with this creature was unlikely, if only for his own shortcoming.

Eventually, he realized he didn't have a choice. If he was going to get his talisman back, he had to kill again.

He recalled what he'd unwittingly said after the vulture's demise, and he reiterated it here; this time prior to destroying this creature.

"I'm sorry." He said lowly, but that wasn't good enough.

"I'm sorry!" He cried, and he hefted the stone as high as he could. The snake tracked the stone's movement. It could sense what was coming, but it did not give way. It would not.

"Become me!" The serpent seemed to be telling him, staring baleful into his eyes with a machine-like cold intent. It wanted to die, he felt. It wanted to die, on purpose. This confused him. He hesitated. He almost stayed his hand, distrusting the serpent. But the beast was insistent.

"Kill Me." It dared.

With a heave, he thrust the stone at the beast in the bush, but it was heavier than he knew even as he'd carried and threw. And his inexperience was paramount. His aim was resultantly terrible.

It fell just short with a thump. The snake struck at it, so swift the man didn't even register it until after the fact. But the stone's throw had momentum enough. It bounced once, although only barely in the softness of the sand, and rolled forth, striking the recoiling rattlesnake and the shrub alike with a snapping of twigs.

The rattling died instantly, but then rekindled and redoubled its fervor like a snuffed flame that refused to die. The bush was still alive and the serpent was struck only a glancing blow as the stone rolled over half of its body and passed. But swiftly the rattler was backing away and aside, sidewinding like liquid power out into the sun to let him witness its full, beautiful terror. He tensed and backed away, but the beast did not attack.

Begrudging his power, it instead gave ground in a hasty retreat. It realized it was overmatched, despite its size and lethal bite. It could not compete with great stones larger than itself which felt no pain and suffered no poison.

Seeing his success, the man quickly scanned the ground underfoot and found many small throwing stones, and he repeatedly, rapidly gathered them up and threw them as swiftly as he could. Many missed their mark. In fact, he couldn't be sure if any ever actually struck death a smart blow, but the effect of the assault was enough. The rattlesnake furiously beat its buzzing tail upon the air, a blur of imagery and sound that the man would not soon forget, but it backed away nonetheless until there was such a distance between them that his stones' throwing was as futile as breathing at the beast.

Luckily, the rattlesnake now realized its location out in the open sun, vulnerable and exposed, and death turned from him, seeking refuge wherever it might find it elsewhere. Finally, triumphantly, the man smiled, reclaimed his talisman, and clutched it dearly to himself. Fear fell away almost entirely. He had conquered it on his own, and somehow made peace with death. A begrudging respect had been earned from it, and a healthy caution and respect for it had been learned.

He reminded himself, grateful that he hadn't had to kill it, to be on the lookout for it in the future. That way, he could find a way to deal with it before it became necessary to kill. He felt in that moment, a great importance in not only problem solving, but in the rudimentary but growing sense of what other right minds might label as philosophy; particularly in regards to conflict resolution, which gave birth to the notion of perspective and paths, and the effect choice would have on them both.

There was always a better way to solve disputes of any kind than killing.

In this case, he'd just thrown some stones, and the problem had gone away, and surely that was the very definition of the use of violence to get what he wanted. That in itself was not the right way to do all things, but sometimes it had its benefits if the cause was just and right, as was his claim to his talisman. But more importantly, he realized it didn't have to come to death. There were *peaceful* ways of solving such dilemmas, and he would remember that just as he would be on the lookout for his old nemesis, his now respected equal, death.

\* \* \*

*He* walked long that day, despite his injuries and the sickness inside of him. Drinking much of his water had helped. But, the weakness in his body and mind intensified rapidly. Delirium settled in more deeply, growing ever stronger. It came in waves, rising and falling, resulting in a long series of dreamlike periods of incoherence broken only by shortening moments of clarity and discovery in reflection and thought. But due to his illness, those inspired moments were disjointed at best.

Although he would feel he learned something or other, time and again, in his increasingly briefer respites from whatever flu had come over him, they were also lost repeatedly when the sickness returned with a vengeance, only to then be rediscovered with his next fit of sanity.

Cyclically, he retreaded the same ground he walked, both internally and in the world beyond the tangled recesses of his mind. Though he couldn't be certain, and though he walked a straight enough line to have gotten somewhere, the world all looked the same and he felt he was spinning his heels endlessly in the same place he'd been that morning.

Night came and went, the only thing that didn't reiterate the futility of his aimless wandering, and he walked the whole way through, freezing and starving once again. He drank the most of his bottle by then, but had at least the presence of mind to keep a reserve.

Somewhere less than a quarter full, it still reflected him.

Soon the world's turning beneath the sun became a part of the not-so-merry-go-round. Day rose and fell anew, night came and went again, and still he trudged onward until everything fell into line, time itself becoming one with the blurring cycle of repetition.

He was caught on a carousel of self. He would be lost here in this new reality forever, he sensed. But even that failed to trouble him after the second night. Helpless, he embraced the sickness, and immersed himself in the crazy haze of thought and sensation until there was simply no discerning one from the other; clarity from insanity.

Soon after that he was little more than an animal, as he'd been when first he'd awakened in this hellish landscape, a thing only stumbling ahead through raw ignorance and belligerence, marching foolish through his sweltering wasteland dreamscape. It was, in essence, yet another new form of reality he hadn't expected; one where both dream and vision were living in the same time and space as his waking hours.

His talisman only seemed to confirm it whenever he glanced to it's glistening plastic. Though he drank periodically from it, not even it seemed to be emptying, furthering his sense that nothing would ever change again.

His reality, once separated into two equally fascinating parts and multiple confusing times, was collapsed together into a single state.

It was bizarre as could be expected.

The land swam and shimmered, not only from the heat-soaked sands casting their mirages, but doubly from the delusions of memories and imagination running wild without him. Interspersed less and less with moments of clarity, he was allowed to witness and reflect on the phenomenon he was enduring in ever shorter glimpses.

He simply roamed, aimed in what he considered the same direction he'd always been marching, but having no way to verify or care if he was or not. The verge of death, no longer even a concern, was swiftly catching up to him. He was entirely unaware, where he'd last told himself to keep an eye out for death in the future, until some untold days later when a moment of clarity caught up to him and instinct reared its brave head once again.

He crested a dune and came to a staggering halt. The high sun burned down upon him, drying him out so completely even his talisman failed to spare him.

He glanced to it in his hand, prepared to take a drink as he rested and gained his bearings. But it was mostly empty now. He didn't know what prompted him to resist drinking the last of it, but he lifted his hand off the cap before unscrewing it. He simply conceived of *conservation*, rationing himself for the *after*, the future, even as he forgot of the importance of the *before*.

*'Better to save it for when absolutely needed,'* he thought, and he heard his own voice speaking those words, deep and resonant within and without himself. His own voice seemed godly again in that moment, and it startled him. He glanced around swiftly, seeking himself in a bizarre sense that he was not within himself. He was somewhere beyond his body, and yet, attached to it, tethered somewhere within it.

This was a nauseating sensation of the mind, a sensation he'd not yet experienced on this level, nor would he have been able to conceive of such a feeling prior to this moment.

He stared at his hand again where it hovered over the bottle-cap.

It didn't even look like his own hand, so weathered and dirty, so wounded and parched by the struggle he'd endured. It didn't feel like his hand either. Though it was in pain, burned and blistered, cracked with dryness, and had been bleeding in spots; it was also a fuzzy sort of numb, as if it surely wasn't his and he surely wasn't fully within this skin. He felt as though he was from beyond, as though this was all just an illusion and he was just wearing a puppet of himself.

He flexed his fingers, watched them crack and bleed anew where they'd been, but that numbness persisted even as he found it was in fact his hand.

Yet, it still somehow wasn't.

It blurred before his eyes, leaving tracers as he waved it slowly before his face. The tracers hissed to his ears as if the wind and the sands prattling ever-so-finely over themselves as they shifted on the breath of the world.

The fine hiss swelled to a rattle, and he had a vision of the serpent in the bush. Only, it wasn't a rattlesnake smaller than himself. It wasn't either an illusion of the heat, or a vision in a dream. Instead, it was a hallucination with his waking eye, and the reaper came as great as a dragon, a vast, huffing, coiled body that consumed the lay of land itself. It bore a deadly face so big it would swallow him up without trouble. Its breath poured into his body as hot as the desert winds. A single long gust, it filled him with terror.

He recoiled, backpedaled a pace, and screamed his panic.

Death had returned to him yet again, and this time it meant to claim him. Clearly, it had chosen a form that could not fail again.

He tried to clutch his talisman, but his numbed hands refused to grasp. He grappled with that fact just as surely as the slippery plastic, but only fumbled further and dropped the bottle to the sands at his feet. It barely made a sound to his senses as it stuck in his furthest forth footprint and its contents sloshed dimly to rest.

Forgotten in the face of the great viper then, his talisman would not save him now. For some unknown reason, he couldn't bring himself to retrieve it. He didn't even cower. He just stared back at the serpent and saw his end in the rattlesnake.

Its dark tongue flickered out, and it drew such a breath that all the wind in the world reversed itself. Along with it, it swept the sands, as well as the heat of the land. Cold fresh air washed his backside, and he felt pulled upon by it, drawn into the beast. It somehow cleansed him, and he felt no fear, nor weariness. He felt no illness, despite the depth of his fever and his present hallucination.

He reached out for the serpent to take him, as if it was the most rational thing he could do. He was ready to meet his end where a sane man would vehemently fight it to his very last. But such was this moment of clarity, blended with unreality, that he came fully back into himself.

All it took was a blink, and when he opened his eyes, the great figure of death was gone. Its hiss and rattle had been vanquished, and in its stead was a vision he couldn't readily define, though he felt its familiarity within himself.

Far across the sands, shimmering in the heat, was a stand of shining rectangular blocks and oddly shaped spires set against a deep blue sea. For a moment he studied it without comprehending, but with his sickness momentarily dispelled and his mind quiet and clear, he quickly came to grips with the image.

It was a city. Instead of great death owning the landscape, there was this salvation, this civilization. Like in his dreams, skyscrapers lined with windows stared back at him like living things with thousands of dull lidless eyes.

He'd done it. He'd reached civilization.

There would be *others.* There would be communion.

And therein would be knowledge and salvation, not death and terror and isolation. Death had only come back to him now, to say goodbye, to congratulate him on his triumph over its best efforts to claim him.

Slack-jawed and mind-numbed, he stumbled ahead, and left behind his talisman with only so little water remaining. He simply forgot all about it as his moment of clarity carried him toward this new mirage; only he didn't feel it an illusion. This place was real. He recognized it somehow. He'd seen it before.

A short time later, of course, his sickness began to creep back into him and he realized how important it was to reach the city.

He was broken. He was ill. There would be people there. There would be aid. His present salvation, what might come after, and the reclamation of his past alike; all depended upon it.

His instinct to preserve his life was a powerful force. It pushed and pulled at him, forcing him ahead with a single-minded determination. Of course, he was still a very long way off, but he could reach the city, he felt. He would, if it killed him; an ironic thought that was completely lost on him. It didn't matter. He walked on, sensing his salvation at hand.

All he had to do was reach the city, and he would live. Everything he'd thought of achieving by finding *others* was within his grasp. His mate and claim to her. His friends. His acquisition of knowledge and language. His everything lay there on the horizon. All he had to do was make it there.

He didn't even realize he'd overlooked discovering his identity, for to his perception he had already discovered that.

You're Spit would have everything else, though. That was for certain.

So he put one foot in front of the other, again and again and again, and kept pace within himself.

Sooner or later, he would reach salvation.

\* \* \*

*As* he walked, he yet had plenty of time to think, and so he did. But his sickness made it a challenge, even with the beacon of the city hovering there on the sands to guide him.

Triggered by that same beckoning imagery, he found himself pondering his previous experiences and dreams, particularly his godly-self, surrounded by others who beseeched him for answers he couldn't comprehend.

Who were they to him? What did they expect him to give?

He had nothing. Even in that dream, he hadn't possessed anything.

Did they require knowledge from him? And if so, what sort? Did he possess some that he wasn't aware of, from *before*?

At this point, he didn't have but few bits of wisdom and knowing to impart upon them. He felt, if he did have these things to give, possession or knowledge alike, he would give them freely, for those people looked so longingly upon him to have what he offered. Their need was strong and he sensed it was just. He felt it was his duty to give it to them, and not for a second did it cross his mind to ask for anything in return. It simply wasn't in his nature to be that kind of selfish. It wasn't in the hearts of men to be inherently selfish, after all. It was something they learned, though he didn't realize or even conceive that others could and would be selfish just yet. All he knew was his own giving nature.

He didn't see life as anyone else did. His limited experiences and incomplete memories didn't afford him the harsh ways of mankind that had been bred to become the norm of society. But as he thought about giving freely whatever he could to help *others*, all of whom he didn't know and had never met, he was forced to recognize the opposite of himself being a real possibility.

Else, why would they beseech him, whom had nothing to give, in their time of need? Surely still other *others* denied them what they sought from him.

But why? Were they underserving of even the barest kindness? Were they somehow undeserving of even the simplest necessities? Like, *water?*

This was a complex matter to ponder without any experience to measure his thoughts against, and he moved to clutch his talisman to reassure him that he still had his own water, and that he could share it with another if he met those people again and that was what they needed. It was all he had to offer, after all. But he found his hands empty and his talisman lost.

*85*

Strangely, he didn't panic. He now recalled leaving it behind, and he felt he knew why he'd cast it aside. He'd outgrown it. Not only that, but he simply hadn't need of it anymore. He was going to reach the city, meet others, and learn and live his life beside his woman. Things were going to be okay without it.

The vision of his godly self, the sound of his own voice, internal yet filling the world beyond his body, and his conquering of death all pointed to this fact of his talisman's absence.

He hadn't lost it. He'd cast it aside. He'd moved *beyond*. He did not mourn its loss. He had learned much from it. It had told him who he was, to himself and to the world. It had saved him. It had defined the world for him. There was no more purpose for it. He had filled himself with that purpose, having drank it, and once that had happened, he saw now how the talisman had actually held him back. Once he'd surpassed it, it had become a liability, and almost led him to his death at the fangs of the rattlesnake.

He lifted his chin proudly, glad now to be rid of it. It had been a crutch, and though it had helped him, led him, filled the universe with his sense of self and purpose and connection, it had only been a burden in the end. It had been a delusion, a false idol, a belief, and a foolish one at that; not a magic bauble.

He was so much more than only that much water. He was so much more than a container. He was You're Spit. He was a god. He was the all, and the all was within him. The talisman was just like everything else in that sense. It was just a part of him, a reflection, a reflector, an instructor, a guide.

Strangely, he had a sense that he'd been holding himself back in placing so much faith in an icon. He needed no icon. Certainly not one which he rationally knew now was just a common bottle of water.

The city loomed before him, and he'd found a way out of the desert and overcame death on his own. The icon was folly. He would never follow another now. He was all he ever needed, in and of himself. Perhaps, he suddenly realized, that was what the others beseeched of him. They sought to be of him, as was only befitting of a god. Though, immediately he recognized, they were all of them, one and the same. That was why he felt he would give to them so freely, for they were all together in this reality, this life. Bound together by the all, and being of it and containing it; they were all *him* as well.

His mind almost cracked at that massive consideration. He felt the weight of the all pressing down upon him at that realization.

*There was no salvation*, his senses screamed at once.

There were no others. They were all the same, one and another. There was no struggle. There was only the dream, and the real, and even they were bound together within him, existing now simultaneously as he walked toward this beacon.

The *before* and the *now* and the *after* all blurred together. The memories and the reality and the aspirations. His friends and his lover and the others. His sickness and his clarity. His waking and his dreams. The day and the night. Life in all its forms, and death itself. Everything was one and the same.

It all just instantaneously collapsed for him.

He blacked out. His senses simply refused to continue.

Perhaps it was the sheer weight of what he'd just reasoned through. Perhaps it was the heat of the desert. Or maybe he was simply that ill, and the strength of its newest wave was just too much. He would never know which.

But he didn't fall or fail. He simply wasn't home anymore, marching onward, unaware, and he only inexplicably came back to himself when he was standing at the edge of society.

The very edges of the last of its streets stood before him. Right there at the edge of the sand-scape, it simply was, and it waited for him.

He swayed there, sickened to the point of barely recognizing these things he'd never actually seen with his waking eyes before.

His dreams had done nothing to show their true grandeur in the real.

Likewise, they'd done nothing to show their true ruin.

* * *

**The** street he'd arrived at ran right up against the scrub and sand of the desert. At his very feet, the sands dwindled onto concrete. He hesitated, afraid to step forward from the curb.

Clarity had returned, but he couldn't be certain this was so. No longer was anything for certain. He'd marched for so long, experienced so much, that he was left forsaking all of his previous discoveries and self-assured truths. Not even what he saw could be judged as real anymore.

Now, he entered a new trip. Now, as he finally reached salvation, society, and others, he was left with an inexplicable doubt for all things. It all prompted a single lofty question.

What was *real* anyway?

He scanned the street that crossed his path. It was desolate. It was a slum, though he didn't know any better. It was ugly. After working so hard to find it, all he could express was a sense of disappointment and disgust.

He grimaced, more from these feelings than the effort it took to keep his feet and continue on in any fashion.

A series of rundown buildings lined the far side of the street. Dumpsters and broken down, derelict cars were scattered intermittently amid the scene. Trashy litter dotted the urban terrain.

The place looked abandoned, empty like he had once been, empty like his talisman. But there was some substance to it all, another reflection of what little he knew. However, there were no people milling about in their personal business.

There was simply no one.

Where were they all? Where had they gone? Why had they abandoned him now that he'd found them?

He then looked up to the greater buildings beyond these nearest, and hope was kindled. Maybe they simply weren't home here. Maybe they dwelt in the more grandiose towers ahead.

He drew a dry and dusty breath and started forward, setting foot onto concrete for the first time. It was solid as it looked, and it made his footfalls dull on his ears.

He crossed the street, passing between the buildings, the foremost of which was a fuel station. Its acrid scent reached out to him, and he shriveled his dry passageways in disgust and pain. Quick to move past this scent, he held his breath until he reached the next street. And still more of the same filled his vision.

It was a desolate, abandoned city. He began to despair, but fought back the tears that threatened to come. He wouldn't let himself believe he was still alone.

He picked his way in a straight line, walking down a single street and taking in his surroundings with a stark sort of awe. The buildings were widely varied in both size and shape, and he marveled at their possible uses. Soon they grew larger still, but still no people showed themselves. The place was a hollow shell, an empty promise. There were no others here. There was no comradery to be found, no joy to experience, nor salvation to be had. There was nothing new to learn, no words to discover, and no hope whatsoever to find his mate, much less reclaim his place by her side and in her possession.

He walked clear across the city, and every step he took pushed him further into depression.

At last he passed cleanly through the mightiest of the structures, and reached the far side. The buildings diminished almost immediately, and gave way to a concrete boardwalk, beyond which was only more sand, and then the far expanse of an ocean of water. Its roar reached out to his senses as its waves crashed upon the golden shore.

There was simply nothing else to see.

Miraculous, such an expanse of water should have been, but his depression was complete and he found no joy in seeing this.

Glumly he began to realize, worst of all the absences here, there would be no *answers*.

He smelled the salt in the sea and listened to the wind, and felt utterly alone. He couldn't believe it. He'd walked all this way, and reached nothing.

The tears started to come of their own accord though he had none that he could afford. Salty, they stung his dry eyes, and he began to sob. Sorrow turned to rage, and he screamed at nothing, releasing his frustration at the lifeless sea. The ocean roared back at him with its crashing waves, taunting him, combatting him, stronger and louder and forever more everlasting than he could ever hope to be.

This was the end of the world, this desolate gray street, and it would be the end of himself as well. He'd only just begun his life, poor You're Spit, but had gone through so much. And all of it was for nothing.

He cursed this city. He cursed the world, and himself. He hated.

Everything. All.

Lost, he cried his illness and agony and madness there on the vacant boardwalk until a white gull appeared. It squawked its shrill cry, drew his attention, and sailed in from over the sea. He watched it, wracked with sobs that would not cease, and tracked it as it moved overhead and into the desolation of steel and glass. He turned around with its passing, and was slapped across the senses by a sudden transformation of all that he'd passed through not minutes before.

The desolation of the city had vanished, and it was a haven of beauty and life the likes of which he'd never imagined ever existed before this moment.

The high skyscrapers gleamed in the sun, pristine jewels each, lovingly and uniquely crafted to stand apart from their neighbors for only the wealthiest of societies. The streets were lined with greens, trees and grasses, flowers and all. Every inch of it was diligently cared for at no small expense.

It was changed before his eyes, a resort city now with no equal the world over. Its wealth could even be smelled. He couldn't place it or name it, but he was somehow familiar with Dubai's gross opulence. He felt as though he'd seen this all before, but he had no right recollection of any of it.

But just like that, and far more importantly, he was no longer alone.

As if the white bird was god, the giver of life and dreams, he was simply, suddenly, in a paradise, a heaven, filled with patrons.

He might have died.

He stepped forward in awe, joy mounting a smile to his grizzly, burned face, and an abrupt and blaring horn stunned him as a shining pickup truck roared past, music blaring out of its tinted windows along with an unintelligible, shouted curse from its driver.

Clarity came fully back to him, and he felt instead of illness, sickened by the abrupt shift in his sense of grounding. He backed out of the street and onto the boardwalk again, feeling solid for the moment.

His eyes flew everywhere, taking in people, vehicles moving to and fro, vendors at fine shops peddling their foodstuffs to waiting lines. He spun with the sights and sensations, and the beach was now dotted by hundreds upon hundreds of people sun bathing and swimming. They filled its expanse from one end to the other, further even than he could see in either direction. Sails and yachts punctuated not a dead sea, but one teeming with life's luxury and revelry.

Relief and confusion swelled within him, and he felt the spinning return and intensify. So many chaotic sensations were pouring into him, so many emotions were welling up within, that he grew dizzy and staggered and fell to his knees.

He was weeping again, but he didn't even register the fact, too stunned by all that he was experiencing.

Was it another illusion? Or had the emptiness of the city been the dream? What was real? Was this a memory? Was it all one and the same?

What was the *difference* anyway?

He was still utterly alone. No one seemed to even notice he was there, or if they did, they didn't care to see him. Worse, they turned up their pretty noses and avoided looking at him.

A couple walked past him on the boardwalk as he knelt and wept, and they veered around him, giving him a healthy berth. He reached out for them, but they avoided him and moved on quickly. They were beautiful people. Everyone here was beautiful and wealthy. Every vehicle was meticulously maintained, shining and clean. Everything here was a thing to be envied and lusted after, but never attained.

He was filled with his prior sense of want, but it took an empty, hollow form. It was not a fulfilling desire, but a false one, this wealth and beauty. It wasn't like his dreams of the mountains and trees and his soulful mate and her lusting, loving eyes. She was no less beautiful than these people, but she was more beautiful in the sense that there seemed to be more to her than these who traipsed around him, avoiding him like a diseased bum; these who were only superficial images shackled in life by their own pursuits to possess and conquer the world's many trappings.

Suddenly, he took note of what he must appear to be to them. He was not the *all* he knew himself to be, and neither were they. He was surely no better than a homeless vagrant that didn't belong. He himself had once treated people like himself, as poorly as these were treating him now. He didn't have a vision of it, but he felt it was true. And he was abashed at his own behavior. He suddenly wondered if the *before* was worth discovering, or if he would just be ashamed of himself.

Being confronted with humanity in its pinnacle leisure, wealth, and hedonistic glory, he was awakened to many things he hadn't previously conceptualized. And none of it was pretty. Certainly, it wasn't so beautiful as its makers wanted him to believe. It was the opposite. It was positively hideous.

As he came to grips with all of it, which was certainly smaller than the *all* with which he had grown familiar and which did not dissipate as so many of his other illusions and greater understandings of all of it often did, he began to collect himself and was filled with the fear. He realized then that his *all* and all of *this* were in direct opposition, and yet this one didn't fade away. His *all* was only imaginary and faded fast. But it also somehow pervaded his very being. It shaped him and molded him, just as this all shaped and molded these people, separating them from him. The question was, which was real? Which was actually forever? Which was true and right to embrace?

He had to know if what he was seeing was real or not. He had to make them see him and interact with him, or he would be trapped in ignorance forever and he would never know the answers of the all. He staggered to his feet and stumbled at the nearest pair as they walked by.

"Help!" He managed a new word on need alone.

"Help me." He muttered, reaching out for the man. The fellow was as richly appointed as the setting, jeweled and dressed in fine, formal, designer clothing. He came complete with a fancy, shiny hairstyle and big sunglasses to protect his eyes from the light.

He flinched away from You're Spit, and when You're Spit pressed his approach, the man grappled with him, revolted, and then shoved him to the ground as if he despised to be touched.

"Get away from me, you homeless fuck!" He kicked You're Spit after he was on the ground, and the helpless man curled into a ball and sobbed.

"Ugh!" The man shuddered, and his beautiful, scantily clad, tanned sex object of a woman laughed as he pulled her along.

"Get a job!" He called back as they moved off.

"I'm going to get a disease!" The man then said to the woman.

"Where's the police when you need them? They need to do their jobs and get rid of this pile of shit." She answered. The man moved to turn back, winding up a kick again, but his woman dragged him along.

You're Spit cried, unable to defend himself or express himself and he didn't understand what he'd done wrong. He didn't fully comprehend the man's words, nor his woman's, but some of it stung as if he did.

Was this what he'd been through sand and death to reach? Why?

He'd been better off in the nothingness, alone with his talisman and death for company.

He suddenly regretted forsaking his bottle and the all it had reflected in his reality and self.

*Judas.* He didn't rightly know the name's full connotations, but it echoed in his mind, heralding him as a traitor, even unto himself.

\* \* \*

*Some* painful tears later, a shining police car rolled up. The officers got out, and he looked up to them. They were menacing figures with features contorted in disgust.

"How'd he get this far into the resort?" one asked.

"Who cares? Put your gloves on. Let's take out the trash."

They didn't so much gather him up as they did rough. He fought them, but he was weak despite his wildness. His flailing only pissed them off. They beat him harder, subdued him, threw him into their air-conditioned vehicle, and drove him away.

Several times he pleaded to be heard, but all he could muster was his prior plea.

"Help me!" he tried, but they only shouted back.

"Shut up!

They drove him through the city, and he succumbed to silence, watching it all pass by as he thought of ways to get them to understand him. If he could only speak well, and tell them his story, he thought they would understand. But he feared trying that after their beating and harsh refusal to hear anything he would say.

One thing came of his ride that was positive above the cold air afforded by the machine's cabin. He now knew he was not dreaming. This was the real. His all was a farce. He had reached salvation. But, it was unexpectedly rejecting him.

Soon, the police deposited him back roughly where he'd originally entered the city, far on the other side of all the high, elaborate buildings; all of which took on new beauty as they were colored with life. Then, they got back in their car and drove away, leaving him at the edge of the desert to die. Lost, again, he just watched them go, and remained where he was seated in the blistering sun for many long minutes.

Across the street, at the gas station, a man stood in the doorway and watched him. He hugged himself and felt so alone. Again, he sobbed his desolation, burying his face into his knees until a shadow eclipsed him.

He sniffled back his salty tears and looked up. It was the man from the gas station. His face was seamed with age and browned by not the sun, but by his genes, though You're Spit didn't know the difference. He had a bottle of water in his hand, and You're Spit licked his cracked lips, immediately assuming it was his own bottle of water at first. The man offered it to him, squatting down before of him.

*Such a kind man, to return his lost talisman.*

"Here you go." he said. "Don't worry about paying."

You're Spit took the bottle without hesitation. It was ice cold in his hand. Hastily, he unscrewed the cap and drank, grateful for the kindness in this older man. It was so cold he gagged and choked on the refreshing shock it poured into him, but he muscled through it and drank desperately, feeling his emptiness again.

"Thank you," he croaked, stricken by pain and brain freeze, and surprising himself with these new words of gratitude.

"Don't mention it," The man spoke, and You're Spit noted his peculiar middle eastern accident.

"Just stay out of trouble. Don't know what you did, but I've seen them beat people out here, badly. Most of them far better off than you." He made it a pointed statement.

You're Spit realized he looked like he'd been through hell, and he had, so the foreigner's message somehow didn't get lost on him. He was beginning to understand words better. Just being around others, even when they spoke little, jarred something loose in him. He felt like he could almost speak like them if he just had more time to listen.

"What's your name, my friend?" the man asked when he made no move to rise or speak further. It took You're Spit a moment to decipher what the man was asking, but something in the man's word-use caused him to twitch.

*My friend.* That part rippled through him in a way he couldn't define. It made him shiver.

When he finally deciphered the man's words beyond that jarring figure of speech, and he understood the question, his eyes lit up. He knew his name! He could communicate it! If he opened his mouth, he was having a conversation; his first ever!

"You're Spit!" he blurted eagerly, smiling, and the man looked at him, incredulous. He didn't realize the insult for what it was. Seeing the man's face shift from surprise, to calculating, and then turn swiftly into a look of displeasure, he feared he'd said something wrong.

"You're Spit!" he tried again, struggling to rise, but the man looked furious and backed away as he rose much faster than You're Spit could muster. He reached for the man, desperate and confused, but the gas station attendant kicked him back down just as the finer man had done before.

"That's the thanks I get?" he muttered, but You're Spit didn't catch much of it.

His head struck the concrete curb when he fell, and lights sprang up behind his eyes.

*'Please,'* His mind whispered, but his mouth failed to respond. *'don't think so poorly of me.'*

* * *

*"Please,* don't think poorly of me." Adam Penhale stood before his board of directors, all of whom wore looks of disbelief. His placating hands brought silence to fill the room. The large banks of windows to his left shed angular golden light on the proceedings, giving the modern decor a new sense of life.

He remembered it strongly now, feeling cleaner even than it looked, but as it had never felt before. This morning was his day of freedom, and he breathed in this acrid air-conditioned environment, so sterile, as if a welcome forest's breath. He wouldn't be here for long, and that lifted his spirits even higher than they'd been when he'd made his decision.

No one had anything to say to his revelation, though someone coughed in an effort to ease their discomfort. The black glass table between them all reflected their eyes. They couldn't even look at him.

In truth, he'd expected this sort of response to his proposal. Naturally, it wasn't a choice one would make in their right mind. Though, it didn't also affect the company. It wasn't a business decision he'd announced, at any rate. It was a personal one. It was a shocking one. It was only because he was the company's owner that it would affect the business and its relative stock values. He couldn't quite remember its name, much less what he'd built it to be. He couldn't even recall what it was his company did anymore these days, so severe had his break become, but it didn't matter. It so completely didn't matter to his newfound enlightenment that he didn't even bother trying to remember any of it.

He was distancing himself from it publicly so that it wouldn't be affected by his personal choice. It wasn't as though his company was a gigantic conglomerate worth billions, but it was worth quite something and he'd built it with his own two hands. He'd achieved a measure of success with it and with his life, and now he was casting it *all* aside.

None of them could figure out why. He couldn't blame them. Though he knew exactly why he'd come to his decision to step down from his position, he wasn't going to share it with any of them. It wasn't for them to know.

No one could know. Not yet. He'd lost his mind, or maybe he hadn't, quite some time before this morning. Naturally, he felt what he was doing was brilliant. He didn't feel out of his mind. In fact, he felt enlightened. He was beyond this world anymore. He wasn't going to play by its rules anymore either. He was done, and in parting, he had something to say. He would act accordingly, and give the world his message. In fact, renouncing his position as the head of his own hard-won company was the first message he hoped to send. It would be his fork upon his champagne glass, calling all eyes and ears upon him.

The men and women of the board looked as shocked as he expected them to be, and some even looked sad. He didn't understand that, aside from the fact that they had all known each other for so many years. But it wasn't like he was going to go home and hang himself. He was simply relinquishing what he'd worked so hard to build. And he had worked very hard in his life to achieve this reward. He'd struggled just like any other middle-class citizen to break free of the lower rat races, but now none of that even mattered. He simply called it an early retirement.

It wasn't that difficult to understand. Of course, for them, he reasoned, it was impossible to comprehend. In this world, money and hard work was all anyone knew anymore. Even if they were aware of more than these trappings, and engaged in them as often as they could, they were still trapped by them, governed by them, enslaved by them.

How could he willingly surrender what he'd worked most of his life to attain when he'd succeeded in overcoming those same trappings?

"No one has any questions for me?" he asked of their silence. Several glanced at him and looked away again swiftly. A few managed to stare at him, bewildered, his revelation still sinking in.

"You're just going to sit there?" Tom Lin asked, an aging Chinese American man with a gentle air about him that always made him feel grandfatherly and likable. But make no mistake, Tom was a marketing genius and ruthless toward competition.

Adam scrunched his face, reality blurring between future and past and all. He tried again, but couldn't recall what any of their products were anymore these days. He caught a whiff of arid desert sand, and his vision blurred slightly.

"Just sit there and do nothing?" Tom asked again. "And take nothing with you?"

"That's right. I'm done. I've gained enough. I'm going to sit and do nothing. The permits are already approved, but once the media catches on, I won't even need those anymore. No one will stop me from doing nothing."

"But I don't get it," Sandra Daling cut in, roughly across the table from Tom, but further away. Her dark hair, little less than shoulder length and curled under at its ends, was streaked with gray nowadays. She'd been with Adam's company for twenty of her better years, and they had passed beneath his protective wing as she rose in the ranks.

"I don't expect you to," Adam smiled. "Nor do you have to. Nothing changes for you, unless I'm successful and the madness stops." His words were met with a collective scrunching of features. They didn't understand without any given context.

*'Madness?'* Their eyes questioned it of him and each other.

"I'm just choosing to do something about what I see. It won't reflect on any of you. It won't affect this company. I'll make it known. And you all still have your jobs. I'm just leaving."

And he'd done just that. He'd left his company in the hands of a very capable, very confused group of others.

Of course, there had been backlash.

\* \* \*

*"How* can you do this?!" Jennifer Penhale shouted. She hadn't been able to get much more out; her confusion and heartbreak and fear for her financial security and all of their lives together all stumbled over each other in an effort to be heard first.

Multiple times, she'd tried to argue and reason with him before he'd go to his board meeting on the morrow to do what he felt he must. For days it had been the same battle between them. But she always sputtered out incomprehensible curses and flabbergasted exclamations that didn't hold any water.

His mind hung up on that word for a moment.

*Water.*

He could smell the lushness of rainfall for an instant, but his thoughts quickly moved on as he shook his head to answer her question. He wasn't leaving her. He didn't understand why she could be so hurt by his personal choice to leave his career, her safety net, behind. Of course, he did understand, but it wasn't as though he was divorcing her and quitting his job and moving overseas to become a monk or anything. He was simply taking a stand.

Society needed it of him.

He'd appointed himself, and the problem with ideas of the nature which now guided him was that they could not be unthought. There was nothing more important to him than ending the carnage, ending the greed, and dethroning the evil and corruption that had grown to root in the heart of the world. And there was no other way any one man could ever make a difference in such great schemes. Not when those in power would seek to undo him in order to keep mankind happily in their collective hand-basket to hell. And they *would* seek to stop him, of that he was sure.

There was simply no other way. It was important, even over his marriage, which he'd repeatedly tried to reassure her was not over because of a lifestyle choice. But his Jenn, his beautiful, alluring, beloved woman didn't see it that way at all.

"If you do this, I'm leaving you!" she threatened, slamming the bedroom door for the fortieth time in the past few days.

Apparently, it didn't matter to her that he still loved her and would remain forever hers. She cared too much for the worldly possessions, the comfort and luxury his lifetime of toil had awarded him, and thereby her, as his wife. She'd given her ultimatum. There was no undoing that. She would leave him, because he couldn't abandon his newfound purpose in life. And that mentality was exactly part of the problem he was going to fight to change in the world.

People the world over, but particularly in developed countries, and especially in his beloved America, were hopelessly pigeon-holed into upholding all that was wrong with their world, because everyone had to do what they had to do in order to survive according to the rules laid down upon them by their government, whom in turn obeyed the moneyed interests that demanded such control to begin with.

He'd heard this sort of thing many times, though it never really dawned on him until his recent break. All the things people lamented, were the things they also needed. The things required of them just to survive in a system that existed solely to exploit them. Really, he'd been one of them for much of his life as well, as he'd toiled to make a success of himself. He couldn't count how many times he'd pained himself and lamented his woes for having done so, because it was required of him by someone else above him, or by the system beyond them. And then he'd become the one on top, forcing others to lament beneath him. Though, he wasn't really on top, was he? Not really. Not ever.

This sort of mindset hadn't been in him for many years. After he'd achieved a level of security and financial success, he'd relaxed, but there was a time, he could remember, where he might have sounded like an anarchist, if he'd opened his mouth about what he'd felt in his direst times of struggle.

He couldn't count them all, but he could relive them until he died. His lamentations had been that numerous. From the realization that freedom wasn't free, to the notion that one didn't even own their own genetic code; from the illegality of capturing solar and wind and rain water, nature's freely given bounty, to the unfair, bullying tactics and charges they could lay on a cleanly, respectable young man renting an apartment, and many, many more evils masked by the guise of law and order and goodness - these things all, he'd experienced. And there were plenty more to be sure. And they all weighed upon him now, adding up to a great norm of injustices and wrongs in the world at large. But it was still so much more.

The system was broken, but it wasn't just governmental.

It was everyone and everything.

It was the financial institutions. It was the companies, his own included, and he acknowledged his sins - which was why he was going to atone for them. It was the disregard for the environment. It was the social acceptance of leadership undeserving of their power when corruption flowed so rampantly through their many ranks. It was the people. It was, like his *talisman*, all of it. And he himself was not exempt from bearing that guilt.

He squinted as an image of a bottle of water set in the high desert sands came to him from nothing. He wondered why that image came to mind, but blinked it away as he heard Jennifer sobbing behind the bedroom door.

It *was* everything. It had all grown so gross that the world was not simply no longer what it had once been, for that was to be expected as time went on; it was that it had become what it should not ever be.

From overpopulation, to unsustainable living - no matter what little was being done to combat it; the nature of man was dooming itself. Some might argue, he acknowledged, mankind needed to grow exponentially and evolve to get off this rock and explore the galaxy to find other homes. But Adam thought that entirely unnecessary. Earth was sustainable if it was balanced. That was nature. It could supply every man's needs. It would last indefinitely, if allowed to. But it wasn't being allowed to. It could not fulfill the greed.

Surely, steps were being taken toward more sustainable life by some, but not by all. And those few endeavoring? They weren't enough. They were far too little, far too late. They would all be doomed. As they were, as *all* already were.

Worst of all, through it all, the citizens of earth were wasting their lives trapped in their little personal worlds, enslaved to a lifetime of strife and toil and want, unable to live their lives free of fear and want and oppression, in peace, because the world was a giant machine, driven by economic needs rather than human needs. It was all subject to total oligarchy, driven by lust for money and power, fabricated even in times of financial need to force the people to uphold it still further beyond their means or desires. And all the while, everyone had the wool pulled over their eyes, deceived into it all, tricked into perpetuating it. And the final cherry on top...?

It was perpetrated by faceless corporations. It was executed by entities that, if they vanished from the world, humanity would not even miss, because they were not even real, living beings. But, they were granted those rights handed down to sentient creatures like mankind whom had created them.

"Life's not meant to be wasted in toil," he muttered, mostly to himself.

"There is a better way."

"You're crazy!" her muted scream came back at him through the door.

Her sobbing continued. Maybe she was right. Maybe he was crazy. But that's not how it felt from his side. To Adam, everyone else was out of their minds, blinded, and there were few, or maybe many mutes, who saw the fallacy in their upside-down world; a world where the rich ruled like kings, escaping even the most basic laws - like taxes, for example.

Hell, he'd been one of the perpetrators. His company had been one of them in his most recent years. His company had afforded him tax evasion too, the wretched benefits of being wealthy and above a measure of the law, and if not above, then within rewritten laws that made such evasion and profit legal as taking a breath in a park. That made him sick.

To think he'd capitalized for so long that way when others, homeless beggars by compare, were forced to pay? It wasn't right. It was unjust. And worsening the matter, when the bill was paid, the money went to whatever the powerful deemed necessary and never went back to benefit the paying slaves as it was intended. But, that was only just one aspect of what he now saw in his backward world. There were so many more problems, many of them actually great atrocities. Of course, each and every sin, massive to tiny and back again, was still a sin against the world, a mark against man. He would do what he could to make it right again, even if it meant his death.

"I hate you!" Jennifer screamed again to his silence and refusal to even attempt to console her any more.

"I love you," he whispered back. But he didn't just love her. He loved the world. He loved others. He loved his country. He loved people. He always had, even in his more misanthropic moments. Perhaps that was the great irony of his lifetime. Perhaps that was the great irony of all men and women. They both loved and rejected their own world and all of its people, because it was broken. If people truly had a world and future and life worth living, then they would love one another better. It was simply time he proved his love where few others ever did. It was time he be an example instead of part of the problem. And he knew of no other way to prove his love than to show it in a serene grand gesture that would capture the hearts and minds of all who witnessed it, a macabre gesture that would be talked about for centuries; maybe even forever. But he had to act fast before any word got out and they tried to shut him down; for they would, he knew.

He felt a prickle of paranoia, and something which he wasn't familiar with touched him, something akin to the cold wash of the dark desert night air crept up his spine, making his hair stand on end.

Unseen predators would hound him even now. Unseen creepers would seek to tear him down in his noblest of moments. This fact made him bitter.

Of course, they'd try to stop him! His coming, his fighting, meant to threaten them and bring the end of all that they were, all that they greedily consumed. It meant greater change than they were prepared to accept, as none of it would be 'cost efficient', which amounted to the sole practice and principal by which they lived their inhuman lives. All of what he was going to bring required their extinction. Their survival, ironically, was hinged upon their extinction. If they didn't die, they would kill themselves, and take the planet down alongside. But they would refuse, even knowing that.

He spat in their eye in his mind. They'd sooner kill the world, and all of mankind than surrender a margin of profit. And it wasn't just the men in charge, obscenely wealthy and powerful, but the entities that had become of corporations run by boards and shareholders, men and women, all of them and all of each entity much bigger and more important than any business ought to rightly grow. Companies like the government itself.

Sadly, he shook his head, feeling and knowing it was no longer what he'd always believed. It was no longer by or for the people. It was no longer comprised of people hired to represent order and civility, logic or reason, as it was intended. It was but a cash hound with totalitarian control. All of them were, and there was no rebelling against any of them. Not even in voting.

Of course, rebelling was all he could do with his eyes open to it all. In what twisted, disgusting, evil world was a company of such vast wealth and power possessed of rights greater than that of a human being, human beings whom gave it sustenance in the form of money to begin with? How could anyone not see the fallacy of giving a company, an inanimate organized system for earning money, the sort of treatment a sentient being received? Worse, how could they receive better treatment, more benefits, and more rights? How could they be more valuable? They weren't even real!

He'd passed a homeless man several days ago, so thoroughly downtrodden, filthy and reeking, that he didn't even have the strength or urge or sanity to hold up a sign or a cup for donations. Adam had walked right by the man and sneered in disgust; not outwardly, for he tried to be a pleasant, kind man. But still, he'd felt contempt for that lowly creature.

And now, what did that say about him as a human being?

What right did he have to feel as he did in that moment?

He'd been just like everyone else, deeming that poor creature unworthy of so much as the change in his pocket. What made anyone think a company that wasn't even a living breathing person, deserved better treatment than that poor man?

He didn't know, but he was going to work to undo that notion.

He was going to end it all.

\* \* \*

*The* electric buzz of the convenience store's array of lights and refrigeration units careened through his senses. He stared back at the middle-eastern clerk for a long moment.

"Hello? What's the matter, *my friend?*" the clerk asked, a perplexed look smeared across his bearded face. It must have been the third time he'd asked. He looked perturbed, impatient, but also concerned. The person in line behind Adam coughed aggressively, intentionally.

Adam shook himself free of his dazed thoughts. He couldn't quite put his finger on it, but he felt, off. Something was wrong with him. He felt as if he'd just stepped backward in time. The desert wind caught his senses in the cold of the acrid scent of the air-conditioned store.

He looked to the countertop, a single bottle of water resting on it. The register showed $2.09. The familiar middle eastern clerk was waiting for him to pay. The people lining up behind him were waiting for him to pay and get out of their way, but all he could think of was the clerk's voice. His middle-eastern accented words echoed in Adam's thoughts.

"You know, *my friend*, this is no good. This is no better than the tap."

Adam, along with most people, already knew that.

"What?!" he'd nonetheless exclaimed a moment before he'd lost himself. He remembered that much from before his disconnected moment, but he couldn't place why he was standing there, lost. His surroundings weren't familiar, somehow, though he'd frequented this convenience store for fuel, snacks, and drinks for the better part of a decade. He knew Rahid, the clerk, quite well after all these years, or at least he did in passing and idle banter. Whenever he'd bought a bottle of water here, Rahid, though portly, aging, and not exactly the healthiest living man, always remarked on the pointlessness of buying bottled water.

This was not an unfamiliar exchange. Lately, however, Adam had been out of sorts. And then the recollection as to what triggered his thoughtful daze came back to him.

Lately, he'd been answering Rahid's commoner's helpless wisdom on water with news of his own endeavors to reduce his earthly footprint and get out from under the ridiculous expense of prepackaged water, and to a further extent, out from under the thumb of the city's water company.

The $2.09 lingered in his mind's eye, but the numbers in his head went spiraling upward at a frightening exponential rate. He could literally feel the numbers whirring out of control, and he could hear the profits exceeding obscenity.

"That's why I'm building a purifier." Adam had taken to saying of late. But today he'd missed the beat. Today, he was so frustrated, he simply lost it.

He'd spent thousands on rainwater collectors, pipes, purification units, pumps and fittings and faucets to convert his home water system into an entirely self-sustaining, and far purer one. He hadn't previously been concerned with living off the grid of the city-run water systems that supplied everyone across America with their fluoridated, clean water. He hadn't even always been an ecologically minded man, for that matter. But Rahid had turned him on to reading an article not two months ago about America's foolish, wanton use of water bottles supplied by the big refreshment corporations, and from there he'd spun into reading up on the subject of water at large.

In short, he'd found it a charlatan practice. At length, he found it one of the most ridiculously heinous practices of fleecing that he'd ever heard of.

According to the article, Americans used enough water bottles to circle the earth more than five times... *per week.* At the cost of bottles of water, the industry gained billions for what amounted to, by compare, being no different from virtually free water otherwise consumed from a tap at home. He couldn't quite fathom it, but mathematically, and environmentally, the implications were staggering. The cost of a single bottle of water was nearly three thousand times the cost of the same amount of water when poured from one's own home tap.

Adding to this obscene waste of not only money, but plastic, the vast majority of which did not get recycled on the average, ending up in landfills instead, was a nauseating fact. Adam couldn't believe he hadn't been previously aware of it all, nor that the world hadn't been buried by the sheer count of plastic bottles. Much less that there was simply no outrage in relation to such reality. And it only went further even than this gross negligence of the environment and heinous fleecing of the people.

It was worse because the bottled water wasn't only just the same stuff you poured from your tap. It was in fact oft found to be worse for you in a variety of ways. Anything from arsenic to plastic's own venting of its poisonous make-up could be found in a bottle of water that wasn't always also in your tap. Of course, in research, he'd found out tap water had its own drawbacks in fluoride, which he researched and found to be less than positive. Tap water itself, while less harmful than bottled water, was still not very good for the body, given all that was added to it to keep it "pure" and "clean". It was basically, slow poison and sedatives when compared to real pure spring water from the earth.

And it only got deeper from there.

Even in times of drought in California, huge companies were sucking up, bottling, and shipping that water *elsewhere* to be sold at their ridiculous profit margins, destroying an already decimated water supply for the sake of a buck.

It was baffling. It was *madness*. The fact that he had been unaware of it all, only confirmed to him how much of a complacent, contented, successful, slave of a man, he had become. His vision blurred as he stood there at the counter. He swayed on his feet and felt like he was going to be sick. He gripped the counter hard for stability.

"What's the matter, *my friend?*" Rahid asked him, snapping him free of his renewed trance.

Adam didn't say. He couldn't. Something was wrong.

He shook his head, disturbed, and turned and walked out in a hurry. The world spun for him, but he made it to his car before he felt like retching. He slumped into his seat, slamming his door to shut out the noise of the world.

"What is wrong with me?" He panted, heart racing. "What is wrong?"

His frustration came back to him in the sound of his breath. The resounding failure of his hard work and the complete waste of his money for his water-purification system at home now taunted him. He'd succeeded in building it and putting it to work, but it had failed nonetheless. Oh, it worked perfectly. However, the government came calling not long after he'd freed himself of the grid's supply. He'd been fined considerably for consuming rainwater resources. It was illegal to live free of charge by nature's bounty, he'd found out the hard way.

Not only had he spent a small fortune on outfitting his home, but he'd been forced to hire lawyers and combat being sued by the system, spending another fortune, only to lose and then be fined anyway on top of it all. They even threatened to jail him, and it was all his lawyers could do to keep him out of jail in the settlement of his crime.

His *crime?!*

He wanted to scream.

It wasn't even the money that troubled him. He had plenty and to spare.

It was the entire system. It was so completely broken, he decided then, that he had to do something about it. And so, he'd taken to researching. He didn't bother trying to find a way to reinstate his right to use the rainwater. That was too small for him. Now that his mind was reawakened to the troubles in the world, spawned by a single cause, he'd begun to read everything he could on any perceived injustice.

Today, it all caught up to him, and he had this resulting break.

He'd studied up on environmental matters first; deforestation effects, global warming, unhealthy oceans fraught with litter islands and dead zones, oil slicks and vast irradiated swathes, and even sun-bleached and lifeless coral reefs, all carefully figuring into the equation of polar ice and permafrost thaws and greenhouse gasses. And all of it looking quite bad in the greater scheme of things.

Then he moved on to the financial crooks that made up all the powerful companies and people in the world when he tried to uncover why nothing was being done about the environmental issues. He read articles on banks, the fraud that was the stock market itself, and the fleecing of the people in the form of bail outs and tax cuts for those who didn't deserve or need them - those whom had caused financial crisis' to begin with.

He read up from there on treachery in the government, from alleged and artificial terrorism, false flags, inside jobs and insider trading, to illegal fund raising, vote rigging, gerrymandering, lying, and bribery made legal in the form of lobbying - all of which profited every crooked bastard involved so very much that even just the actions of one in the many made Adam's own entire lifetime of hard, honest work seem puny and foolish.

And after that, he turned to matters that affected the lower citizens of the world. He found out about great trouble in the farming industries, notably, the genetic alteration of the world's cash crops and animals. From practices that lead to mad cow disease, to cloning, to the death gene implanted into patented plants; plants which could be a major source of cancer, and which, if loosed on the world and allowed to crossbreed with nature, could essentially wipe out the world's cash crops in a single generation. From there, things led his reading to the bullying and lobbying tactics which farming and poison-making giants used to get their products implemented as the norm even though they were terrible, as well as implemented to get their profits extracted from the public. And from there, he spilled easily onward into all the policies being implemented to justify and legalize all the corruption and injustices, not just to men, but to the planet itself.

Not everything he read was pure. Much was subjective. Some was unfounded. Some was crackpot conspiracy. But a great deal of it was also very much real. And overall, even a layman like himself in most of these topics could piece together what was unbiased, what was clearly aggrandized, and what was most obviously written with a greedy or partisan political agenda.

Typically, the distinction between the one and the all, truth and fiction, was easy to spot even amid all the misinformation. Generally, anything he read that was in favor of the madness he saw in the world, was brazenly and clearly written with the agenda of greed and maintaining the current norm, written so that things wouldn't have to change and profits wouldn't be lost. He threw aside the subjective, embellished writings as simply sensationalist one way or another. But he kept the scientific reads as unbiased. *That* knowledge was pure, and its interest was only in upholding and showing truth.

There was no agenda behind the science. It was simply truth. And the truth was, the world had gone positively mad. All of it was connected. All of it maddened him, until at last there was nothing left to do but settle on a plan of rebellious action. And he now, sitting in his car outside of his local Seven-Eleven, settled on that plan quite quickly. It was an easy decision to make. In fact, it came to him of its own accord, straight out of the ether of all of it.

Attacking these problems was impossible. He would be denounced, because that was what they did.

"Experts" would be bought and paid for and they would speak against him, against the evidences of their own fields of study even, and nothing would change. Greed would outweigh common sense, logic, or even truth unto the end of all things. One man could not attack these evils, not even a man with some measure of success in their covetous world.

All he could do then was free himself of its tethers and spend his money wisely on causes deserving. He would spend it all. He would forsake his lifetime of hard work, and he would take a stand in the only way that would ever matter.

He would make it a public stand in a public place, and he would make it one of complete peace, one which no one could defeat. And he would speak only when asked, and what he would say would trounce the madness.

It was the only way.

\* \* \*

*Without* telling Jennifer, he spent his money, every last bit of it, strategically setting himself up for resigning as head of his company.

He donated it equally to a variety of causes. He gave huge sums of money to nature conservation. He bought a plot of rainforest, thousands of acres from a logging company, specifically for setting aside as a reserve. He set money into place to protect it for a decade, paying up all the necessary dues and taxes that would be accrued for such a landholding, even though it sickened him that such was required and that all he could do was hold it for ten years before his funds would fully dry up.

He donated to reforestation, a sum that would plant millions of trees this year. He donated to wildlife conservation, hoping to aid in the protection of endangered species. He gave to the homeless and the hungry. He gave to innovative clean-up efforts concerning the oceans, and again to preserving the rivers and lakes of America. He gave so much to so many causes, that he was swiftly broke, with the exception of a reserve fund put into airfare for himself, and permits and materials necessary to make his stand in a very public location.

It wasn't the construction of a fenced dais in Times Square, New York, which won him attention. It wasn't his presence in the public there upon that dais either. Not even after he took his seat did he receive any special note, and even then, only in curious and confused passing glances from pedestrians and motorists in that metropolis. Nor was it the news that he'd stepped down from the head of his company and sent a shock wave through both Wall Street and the pockets of his shareholders. None of these won him the public eye. In fact, all of this came late, as he'd acted swiftly.

Rather, it was his mad dash donations that drew attention. The financial world, the corporate world, was moved *after*, as the news of what he'd done soon reached the media. Then, they took note of his philanthropy and of himself, as if seeing him for the first time.

Immediate speculations arose as he was sought for statements but couldn't be found at home or at work. The media reported him missing, and began making up stories about him and his generosity, as they were prone to do about much of anything when they either had an agenda, or simply didn't know the truth. The media, he could have spat at their designation, was just one more thing wrong with the world. But, they did him a great service in reporting on his unprecedented moves. He was aware of it via the tickers and screens that lit up Times Square morning, noon, and night.

Everything played out before his eyes as he sat there on his dais, protected by his considerably long-term permits. He grimaced at the negative speculations on his sanity, and smiled at the buzz that was rising as to his actions and the mystery of his whereabouts.

It took the world two weeks, and it took him two weeks of beard-growth to be discovered for who he was and where he was hiding in plain sight.

Already, he was starving, and kept nothing but a bottle of water with his person. Admittedly, it wasn't exactly an original idea. In fact, he'd stolen it from a great man of peace and civil rights in the past. But, it had been very effective before, there was no reason to think it would not work again.

Below him a small gathering of people had come this day. Many came and stayed for a time, simply watching and waiting for him to speak, but Adam didn't have anything to say. He was fasting, and the sign attached to his fence spoke all the words he could ever hope to express.

"End the Madness" That was all it said, in big, bold red letters easily legible from great distance. His t-shirt said the same, though in black.

Of course, the throngs of people that came and went daily, some staying, some passing after a time, blocked much of his message most of the time. Nor did they know of what madness his simple signage spoke. That was just more fuel for the speculation. It didn't matter that they couldn't understand or couldn't see. The media had already gotten their shots of him, sitting in his t-shirt and jeans and casual hiking boots above the bold statement. He'd seen it countless times upon the huge screens above the streets. And so, everyone else could also see them no matter how many people obstructed the view.

Naturally, since he didn't have anything to say beyond the fact that he was fasting until the madness was ended, the media began to formulate new stories.

It had become a circus of pure speculation, and it was exactly what he wanted it to be. While his message was lost, yet unknown, and his goals were far from being accomplished, the buzz that he was creating was growing so vast that he'd seen news stories on high from as far away as India.

The world itself was taking note at large. He had succeeded.

"Modern-day Gandhi" Was cast out there by someone, somewhere, and the rest of them picked right up on it. And it spread. They were beginning to call him that almost everywhere, and he knew he was winning.

The madness, the wrongs of the world, were not yet being changed, but they would. He swore it. He just had to remain where he was, and starve until it was time to tell them why he was here and just what cause he was fighting for.

So far, he'd seen speculations from many different angles. They made up their stories based on what they knew of him, and most prominent of these things were his position in life and his recent outrageous donations in what amounted to his total moderate fortune.

Reporters spoke to people he knew, new and old. They spoke to financial experts. They plied ecological experts. They spoke to those responsible for suing him for trying to live off the water grid with his home. They spoke to his wife, or at least tried to. No one had any right answers as to what madness his sign referred to. They simply couldn't imagine the scope of his vision, and that was exactly as he hoped it would be.

That was to say, until the reporters spoke with experts and average civilians alike in India. They went, asking what those people thought of Adam's fasting demonstration. Some thought it an insult to Gandhi's name, but others, the smart ones, thought they knew what he was after.

A doctor and yogi Hindu practitioner, a sort of local wise-man there, was quoted as praising Adam, and was the one who actually backed the Modern-day Gandhi notion that had sprung up in the news. He speculated that Adam was wiser than any of the wild stories could hope to sort out, and he had decided he would come to America and seek Adam's council on matters of self and enlightenment.

On seeing that news, Adam finally moved to address those who came and went at his dais. It was well timed, for yet another news crew was there, shooting for yet another day's "fast against the madness."

He'd become such a story, but he needed to finally act before the public lost all interest and simply let him fade into oblivion and die of starvation without ever having heard his story or reasoning or goals.

He raised his arms. It took a moment for onlookers and lone media crew to take notice. But, eventually, they caught on, and at once, they were in a rush to get through the crowd. The crowd itself pressed close, suddenly realizing he was going to speak.

"I..." he started, then hesitated, waiting for the reporters. "I will speak of the madness when the good doctor Pradesh arrives."

The people looked to one another. The reporters looked disappointed. But at least, at last, they had *something* to report other than speculation on crazy Adam Penhale, and the reporter promptly turned to her camera men and began reciting what he said, recording the stories to be played on television as soon as the editing was complete.

Adam rested easy, ignoring the weeks of hunger that was stripping his flesh from his bones. It wouldn't be long now, before the yogi arrived. Whether the man actually intended to travel to America to see him or not would be inconsequential when the man heard what Adam had said. In fact, the Indian government might well fly him over on their own dime to find out just what Adam thought he was doing imitating their cultural hero so brazenly.

It was only a matter of time now.

And it had absolutely nothing to do with India, Gandhi, or Dr. Pradesh in any way whatsoever.

Adam simply felt, it was time.

\* \* \*

"*Why* are you fasting?" the reporter asked immediately, direct and to the point. She was a middle aged, well known woman in the media circles, dressed richly and professionally. Her pencil skirt made sitting alongside the men on pillows arrayed on the floor of the dais an awkward affair for her. Adam wasn't familiar with her, but he could tell by the way she carried herself that she deemed herself one of the most important, and was likely one of the most watched reporters in the country. She thought it a privilege for him to even be graced with her presence and questions, not the other way around. Naturally it should be she who was given the grace to be the only reporter allowed to join him on his dais in his talk with Dr. Pradesh, if at least only in her own mind.

Adam ignored her. She was rich, and she made him sick with her plastic look and excessive perfume and her entitled nature. A woman of her age should know better, but he couldn't blame her. No one knew what he knew. He instead smiled on the Indian man who had made a very long journey to see him. The doctor eased himself into a cushion, crossing his legs and assuming a meditative, casual pose. Adam's smile was sad and weak. The doctor's eyes were sad in return as he took in Adam's wasting figure. He had been a relatively healthy man with an average build not long ago. But it seemed he'd been starving for months at the rate his muscle mass and fat reserves had evaporated.

"I'm so pleased you could join me, Doctor." Adam nodded, extending his hand. Pradesh bowed and took his hand in greeting, giving a more reassuring smile.

"*My friend*, the pleasure is mine," he started. "But, tell me..."

"Why I wanted to speak with you?" Adam finished for him, seeming prescient with his anticipation.

"How was your flight?" he asked instead.

Pradesh shrugged.

"Mr. Penhale, please, if you would. The people want to know what you're protesting..." The reporter cut in, but Adam held up a hand, insulting her as he cut her off.

"Please, sir." Pradesh beckoned to the woman. "I must know. I have come far at your request. Indulge me. Why do you want to speak to me?"

Adam glanced to the woman, then all the people gathered here. Times Square had been closed off to all traffic not afoot. The place looked as it might on new years eve, albeit without all the fanfare and alcohol. It was crammed from end to end with pedestrians eager to hear what he had to say. The media hype had done its job to get its ratings, but it was now working solely for him, against them.

"What are you protesting?" the woman asked again.

"Ms...?" Adam asked instead of answering.

"Amanda Jennings," she filled him in, indignant that he should not automatically know her name. She was syndicated nationwide, and internationally known. His insulting ignorance stung, and he could see it in her eyes.

"What are you starving yourself for?" she pressed. "What is the meaning of all of this? What madness is it that you want ended?"

Adam thought about it for a long moment.

"I wanted to talk to Dr. Pradesh." Adam gestured to the yogi.

"He has asked you to speak to me," Ms. Jennings cut him short.

"Speak to all of us." Dr. Pradesh shifted. He spoke kindly, a gentle plea.

"What are you standing for? Or against?" Ms. Jennings tried once more. He sighed.

"You." He finally answered. "Your kind."

Ms. Jennings looked confused, then taken aback.

"Me?" she scoffed.

"What have I ever done?" she began to get defensive.

"Not you," Adam said. "The media."

The crowd heard this and at once started to murmur, a few even cheered with laughter, crying out against the twisted tongues long existing in the manipulative media.

"Are you implying the media at large is madness? So, you're against the people hearing the stories that matter around the world?" Ms. Jennings attacked him immediately, alluding to him attacking the free press.

Adam shook his head. He refused to answer that. It was a baited question. He'd already said too much directly to her to be heard fairly. He had better do well to remember not to direct conversation at her. He wasn't here to talk to her. She was here to listen to him speak with Dr. Pradesh.

"I'm here for a lot of reasons." He turned the conversation elsewhere, regaining control and stifling any wind she might hope to build.

"I'm not protesting the news, or the media."

"But you just said," Ms. Jennings cut him off again.

At this, Dr. Pradesh raised his hand to quiet her.

"Please. Let the man talk, miss," he said, and the crowd laughed as her loaded questioning was silenced.

"You're here simply to witness," Dr. Pradesh deduced. "I don't think Adam is here to answer any questions. I think he's here to speak, but not to any specific topic that he's directed into. Rather, I think he's here to speak to a specific topic of his own choosing. Frankly, Miss Jennings, I believe that conclusion-jumping mentality is what issue he might have with the media. And if he was to be here in protest of that, then I would venture to say he would not be wrong in doing so."

Ms. Jennings' face lit up red with her embarrassment. She wanted to defend and start a debate, but she had no way to do so without looking like an indignant petty child rebuking an obvious truth.

"*That's* why I wanted to speak with you, Doctor," Adam smiled in earnest. "You see, after weeks of sitting here, starving, watching this country react ignorantly to my plea to be heard in a world that will never hear the smallest voice...it was you who saw something of what I was about. Out of all the people out there, it was only you who guessed I was more than I seemed."

"But you don't deny being called the Modern-day Gandhi?" Ms. Jennings spoke up, picking up the media-manufactured moniker in a desperate plea to retake control of the interview again. Her challenge was obvious.

"You don't understand, Miss." Doctor Pradesh said. "This isn't one of your interviews. Adam isn't here for you to interpret his motives incorrectly. He would be here whether you ever, or never, came. I don't think things would be any different than yesterday if Mr. Penhale here hadn't seen my reaction to his protest. None of these people...well, some of them would be here anyway. But most of them would not have come. The streets would not have been blocked off for all this fanfare. He would be a man, sitting on an island in the chaos of your city. He isn't here to be interviewed. He's here, waiting to be noticed."

"And the world has noticed." Jennings defied him. "And now that we have, we want to know, what he's after. Are you saying it isn't to be known?"

"Of course, it's to be known," Adam said. "It's a protest."

"So, it is a protest!?" Ms. Jennings announced, and the crowd murmured again. It appeared they were growing impatient with Adam and irritated by Ms. Jennings' pestering.

"It is not madness to simply want an answer as to what you're protesting, Mr. Penhale."

"I actually agree," Adam said, smirking as much as he frowned.

"Then, tell us. What are you protesting? The media? What about it? Or is it the state of the ecology? Could it be global warming? The drought in California?" she fired in rapid succession, repeated talking points of late in the media circus prompted by all the speculations in his silence.

"Many have tried to analyze what it could be. We've seen you surrender Pendant Inc. and donate millions to a variety of causes - all of them overnight. You disappeared, but you were here all along and no one knows why. What is it that you have to say? Why should anyone listen to you, if we don't even know what you're after?"

"I'm not after anything. I personally stand to gain nothing by sacrificing everything in my life and starving publicly," Adam sighed.

"And still you haven't given us an answer, and you're the only one who knows why you're here," Ms. Jennings bit the words off. She was getting frustrated as well.

"Ms. Jennings, please," Dr. Pradesh again lifted a gentle hand before turning to Adam.

"Would it help if I asked the question?" He tried.

Adam nodded weakly, feeling the stress melt away.

"It would."

"All right, Adam." Dr. Pradesh smiled in turn.

Ms. Jennings gaped, at a loss as she was entirely cut out where the doctor took over.

"Why are you following in the footsteps of our great Gandhi?"

It was a peculiarly worded question. It was pointed, and yet, laced with hidden meanings. Adam was pleased and surprised at once. He was glad he'd chosen well in who to speak with, for the matters he had to discuss for all to hear, were more than black and white matters. What he had to share was philosophical, philanthropic, and higher-minded than most reporters would ever think to analyze. Ms. Jennings was already a prime example.

"I do not pretend to be a great man like Gandhi. Nor even Dr. King." Adam said. "I may just be a dumb American, but even I know, Gandhi was all of ours. He stood for something encompassing the entire world. He belongs to everyone. Just as Dr. King, and every other great man belonged to the world, regardless of his nationality or religious belief. They were great, for the sake and need of greatness, and greatness of that kind knows no border or boundary."

At that, the crowd murmured approval. Dr. Pradesh looked surprised.

"So that's why you've chosen his method? Because it is peaceful and wise, and it resonates with all men?"

Adam nodded.

"It was the only way."

"Will you continue to fast after this talk?"

Again, Adam nodded pointedly.

"I will not stop. I will not save myself until the madness is ended."

"So, it comes to it," Dr. Pradesh surmised. "Tell me then, my friend, what madness is it you protest, that we might stop it and get you back on your feet again?"

"All," Adam answered.

"All?" Dr. Pradesh asked, arching his dark brows.

"All of it." He confirmed.

"When I was a young man. I struggled to survive, to make ends meet. I saw the world from a young man's eyes. I saw the wrongs committed against man and earth for what they were. But I grew up, gained success, and grew complacent, considering my life's strife was the source of my thoughts. In time, I turned my back to these things. I forgot of them. And now, I atone for my sins."

Dr. Pradesh smiled, understanding, but he spoke otherwise.

"I do not understand, Adam. Your sins are no greater than any other man."

"That's exactly the point," Adam answered. "We are all of us guilty. We created this world. We uphold and perpetuate it's many, many evils. And only we can stop them."

"Gandhi stood up for civil rights. Martin Luther King stood up for civil rights. These men inspired millions to stand up for civil rights."

"I'm simply doing the same thing."

"What civil rights issues are you talking about? Racial injustices which are still rampant in this country?" Ms. Jennings demanded, immediately assuming he was all about civil rights with his familiar peaceful protest tactics.

"None." Adam ignored her, looking only on Pradesh. "And all. Gods know there's plenty of them." He rolled his eyes and chuckled softly.

The doctor's face faded again toward understanding. He did not find it so amusing as Adam tried to lighten the tone of it. Adam sobered himself. This was not the time for amusing jokes or points of view. There was no room for endearing humor, but for that which came organically in the overall situation of it all.

"When I was a young man, I saw the toil I was enduring, forced by the requirements of merely being alive, and I lamented on them. But still I went to work every single day just to pay the bills, because I had no choice. A man has to survive, you know?" Adam continued on.

"They say hard work will get you ahead, you know? But it isn't the hard work that gets you anywhere at all. And so I upheld the atrocities of my culture. I ignored those in need, the homeless and poor, because ...why should I stick my neck out for another man when I could barely keep my own above water?"

"But you're not protesting poverty, I gather," Dr. Pradesh deduced, beginning to get the picture.

"No," he shook his head. "And yes."

"I am guilty of ignoring the needs of others, just as we all are."

"But you aren't fasting for civil rights or class warfare?"

Again, Adam shook his head.

"No. And this is not to take away what greatness those men did for the world by any means. But in this day, action for civil rights is a very small aim when civil rights issues are only tiny symptoms of much greater problems. It is by no small coincidence that I shunned my fellow man because I couldn't afford to help him. As it is for all of us. We stand divided, by no small coincidence, the same non-coincidence."

"I should think you're right. For one alone is weak, many together are strong." Pradesh considered, "Please, continue, my friend."

Adam considered his words carefully now. After this, there was no going back.

Dr. Pradesh beckoned with his hands in the ensuing silence, bidding him continue.

Reflexively, he looked to the rooftops, afraid for just a moment that somehow, someone out there was already aware of what he was going to say, and that person of power was already prepared to put a well-placed bullet in the middle of his talks.

\* \* \*

*Adam* drew a breath and let out a dangerous sigh to steady himself.

"When I was young, I was rebellious, as many young men are. I have long since outgrown that rebellion. But I see now, I saw then with clearer eyes. Or at least, at the time, the shroud of wool that society tries to pull over our eyes, was only gossamer thin, and I saw right through it."

"Most of us outgrow our rebellion, lulled into a sense of order, controlled, and made to feel as though things are somehow, just good enough. And for the most part, much of them are. But the problem is...things are never truly good enough."

"Explain," Pradesh beckoned with a rolling wrist, looking quite thoughtful with his hands on his chin, and his elbows resting on his folded knees. He looked like a chess master, anticipating his enemy's moves.

"Things can *never* be good enough. We as people, are each of us, incomplete. Like this bottle of water." Adam said, holding it up and setting it down again, most of which he'd drank. "It is mostly empty. We are the same. We seek knowledge, it fills. We seek love, it fills some more. We achieve things, and again it fills a bit more. But a man can never be truly full. For he and the world also drink from its contents."

"We are each of us comprised of only that much water..." Adam drew a breath to steady himself.

"...no matter how full we get. Even should we have more than we will ever need, and we overflow, our container can only ever hold that much water."

"I understand." Pradesh nodded.

"...But *together*, we comprise a vast ocean, a power undiminished and indivisible, a power interminable and incorruptible, by the evils of the world...a power unparalleled by ignorance, hatred, greed or subjugating injustices..."

"...A power of Love. Love for one another. Love for our countries and peoples. Love for the world at large. Love for ourselves. And love for All."

Adam had to rein in on himself. He was revealing too big a picture too swiftly. He needed to remain small and indistinct until it was time to finish this, but it was a challenge to bring himself back down to earth once he'd opened the door to the higher point.

"...no matter how empty or full we are as individuals, we become unstoppable. Our wildest dreams become reality. Unless, of course, that evil takes root within us, or undermines us, or divides us, or twists our aim...as it most certainly, unquestionably *has."*

"Thus, the only question is, what sort of world do you want to live in? Do you want to live in this world, with war and immanent destruction a very real possibility, only due to deliberately fabricated infighting? Or do you want to live in peace and prosper and be happy and contented in a paradise without end?"

"I would certainly prefer the latter," Dr. Pradesh was amused, and he chuckled. It was not a question. There was no real choice to make there. The answer was self-fulfilling and automatic. As such, it was basically idealistic rhetoric.

"You and everyone else, Doctor, literally." Adam nodded. "And together, we can make it so."

"What evil prevents this, then?" the doctor asked. "If not a civil rights injustice, media yarns, or the suffering of poverty, what evil do you protest?"

Adam hesitated, looking up from the doctor to the sea of faces gathered around their talk. He glanced at the reporter, Ms. Jennings, who was hanging on only to get her story anymore. He could tell she wasn't tracking as well as could be expected of anyone else, or simply didn't believe in idealist fairy tales and pipe dreamers. It wasn't her fault. She'd been programmed, just like everyone else, to disbelieve.

"Well, not surprisingly, that evil also starts here." Adam said, laying his hand atop the bottle of water as it sat before him on the dais floor.

"I'm sure you're aware of the filth that has become of our oceans."

Pradesh nodded. "I've heard there are islands of trash, just floating around out there. Even one as big as yer Texas." He mocked an american southern accent poorly enough to make Adam chuckle.

"That's pretty good." He commended the poor mockery with a grin. "But is there anything being done about them?"

Adam's question went unanswered.

"Did you know America alone burns through millions upon millions of these bottles every single week. And but a fraction of them ever even get recycled. Where do you think these non-biodegradable things end up? Landfills? Our oceans? Everywhere? And that is but the tip of the *iceberg."*

He scoffed.

"Speaking of which...do you think *those* will be around much longer to speak of? Or will they pass into fairytale when all the world has grown too hot for ice of any kind?"

"So it is crimes against nature you deem evil and madness, and wish us to unite to end?" Pradesh asked, but once more Adam shook his head.

"No." He answered, and as before. "And yes. But there is more."

"You do know what you're up against? Many do not even believe Global Warming exists - not even with science urging us all to act to forestall its coming. Your own politicians even voted it to be untrue and back out of accords when things are aimed to unite everyone against the potential dangers."

It was Pradesh's turn to scoff at the arrogance of men who thought they could simply vote something away on ignorance or lobbying, on greed, really. Personal profit for the profit of others at the sacrifice of things they deem unreal in their ignorance or stubbornness or both combined.

Adam nodded. "I understand that very clearly, yes."

"Then what more is there that you would share?"

"So much more," Adam answered eagerly, grinning. "As I said, my rebellious youth passed, and I was preoccupied with life, striving for success, blind and lulled by the wool thrown over the wolf with which I walked and then became myself."

"But I'm seeing things much more clearly these days, and my rebellion was nothing more than a product of the internal knowing of right from wrong. I wasn't rebellious for the sake of rebellion alone. As are none of us. We rebel when we feel inherently unjust, evil things surrounding us, guiding us, pretending to protect us...but shackling us."

"The dog bites his cruel master?" Pradesh summarized, and nodded his understanding.

"Precisely, yes. But if you deceive the dog with treats, and teach him tricks, his mind is distracted from the harsh lessons of obedience he is forced to endure in order to become a model servant...or a model...citizen."

Gasps rose up from the crowd, a murmur of approval rippled through them. Ms. Jennings at his side was suddenly distracted by something, and her camera man quit filming long enough to grab her arm and lift her up.

"We have to go," the crewman said lowly to her.

"Dr. Pradesh," Adam said. "We might have to continue our talk tomorrow."

"They're shutting you down," Ms. Jennings whispered harshly, her tone alarmed by the sudden change things had taken.

Riot police had filled Times Square's borders, and a wedge of them was coming up to his dais, pushing and shoving their way through the throngs. The people began to protest, booing the officers. Some pushed back, and those that refused to move promptly paid the price with violence. This nearly incited a real riot, but Adam lifted his hands and everyone looked to him. He sat still otherwise, and did not move.

"Don't stop filming," he muttered to Ms. Jennings' camera man.

The police gained the dais, and a ranking officer of some sort or another produced a megaphone as others menaced the motionless figure of Adam Penhale.

"This demonstration is over!" The officer announced.

"The hell it is!" some angry New Yorker shouted back.

"Disperse and go back to your homes. This demonstration is over!"

"You're under arrest," another officer was fast at threatening Doctor Pradesh.

"You sure you want to do that?" Adam asked.

"Shut up! You're next, Penhale." The officer sneered.

"No," Adam defied him.

"What did you say?" The officer asked, turning to menace him.

"I said, No, officer," Adam answered clearly. "You see, I have permits. I have a right to be here. And nothing I say need actually be taken as truth. I'm merely exercising my freedom of speech."

The cop hesitated, surprised at the calm and logic Adam confounded him with.

"You're conspiring to incite a riot," The officer sputtered. He had his orders, no doubt from someone most unhappy with what little Adam had said thus far, but he knew Adam was right. He couldn't legally arrest the man. He would be free again in a day, and could file a counter suit if he wished. The officer turned back to Pradesh.

"Get up, Doctor. You *can* be arrested."

"Again, officer, are you sure you want to do that?" Adam warned.

"Think about it, sir. The entire nation of India will be watching this on their televisions tonight. Doctor Pradesh came here to speak with me, for whatever reason, and he is my peaceful guest. If they see you arresting him after he's been invited, and done no wrong, you don't know how deep a hole you'll find yourself in when the backlash comes. And make no mistake. It will come."

"Let him speak. Let him speak. Let him speak." A slow chant was beginning to spread, gaining ground over the officer's megaphone and repeated efforts to get the crowd to disband. But there were simply far too many people and far too few of New York's finest to do anything about them without resorting to extreme violence. And Adam was certain neither the mayor, much less the President of the United States, wanted to see anything of the sort taking place.

"Let him speak! Let him speak!" The crowd continued unchecked.

"You see," Adam winked. "You actually work for us. You work for me. It is *we* who employ *you* to protect and serve *us*. You should be defending my right to be here, not trying to take that away from me."

"Do you really need to be giving the lesson still, right now?" Dr. Pradesh found the talk unnecessary in this moment, but Adam had actually expected this to happen. He glanced knowingly to Ms. Jennings' cameraman. This moment was exactly why he needed the camera to continue recording during this confrontation. The police-state that had been growing of America was also part of his protest. These fine, brave people were employed by the people, given badges and weaponry and a fraternal brotherhood to safeguard the civilian population, not to do the bidding of higher masters and punish the people who've done little wrong to anyone. It was a note he would not otherwise find a way to implement in his talks with Dr. Pradesh without sounding anti-police, which of course, would upset a bunch of more conservatively-minded people without them even realizing the point he was trying to make.

Careful maneuvering was required concerning the noble professions of those who worked in the realm of protection, both stateside and abroad alike, both police and military. These professions deserved the respect and reverence Adam felt for them, but they also needed a reality check and a solid reminder of just why they did what they did, and for whom it was supposed to be done.

Finally, the threatening officer relinquished, moving to silence the megaphone with a touch to the other cop's shoulder. Their efforts had been thwarted, for now. It was they who would incite a riot if they persisted.

Adam wondered if they even knew why they'd been called in. He doubted they did. They were just like everyone else in America...blindly following orders. It wasn't their fault.

When the cops began to retreat, the people let out a cheer and celebrated their victory. Adam's hold on their attention grew three-fold in that moment, but when he tried to stand to calm them, his body was too weak to make the journey to the front of the dais.

"Pradesh, my friend, would you help me?" He asked, and the good doctor reacted quickly, rising to help him to his feet, whereupon he shuffled forward to the edge of the dais on Pradesh's shoulder. He lifted one hand, and for a second, he smelled the dust of a desert as if he had somehow felt it before. He felt dehydrated and dizzy. The sun careened down through the buildings.

The crowd quickly quieted, but when Adam went to speak of his need for their silence while he shared words with Pradesh under the eye of the cameras, he felt the world spin. His eyes rolled back and he felt weightless. His vision blurred and went white, and he collapsed.

\* \* \*

*Only* Pradesh's grip saved him from falling flat on his back, unconscious. The crowd roared in worry, but Adam was not gone entirely. The good doctor looked over him, worried as well, but with water and shade and a resting position, Adam recovered in a matter of minutes. He waved to the crowd to assure them he was as well as could be, all things considered.

"You must be careful." Pradesh insisted. "In your weakened state, exerting yourself could be the death of you. I know I can't convince you to eat and break your fast, but I can remain with you and watch over your health to the best of my ability, Adam. You must rest now, or risk another episode. And I won't lie, my friend. The next one could be your last. There's no way to say how much damage you're doing to your body without running tests and knowing your medical history or lifestyle."

"It's about like any other American man's," Adam joked dryly.

The doctor eyed him.

"Then it most certainly will be your last."

Together they shared a laugh. Dr. Pradesh's was considerably heartier than Adam's own.

"If you would like, I could ask the people to disband and come back tomorrow to finish our talk," Pradesh offered.

Adam shook his head.

"No. We might not get another chance here. You've seen what has already happened, and I've only just begun talking."

"But you have the permits. They can't well make you stop."

"I have them for the next three months, yes. But obviously, I won't last another three months of starvation, will I doctor." Adam eyed him pointedly.

Pradesh smiled sadly, then shook his head. "No, I don't suppose you will."

"Is that your professional opinion?" Adam smiled lopsidedly.

"You're an interesting man, Adam. I should have liked to have met you many years ago."

"You've met me now," Adam answered. "No time like the present."

"None. Agreed," the doctor nodded, looking down to his hands.

"Besides, you wouldn't have liked me as I was, many years ago." Adam gave him a sad look, and he let the guilt he felt for all that he was in his life show through his eyes.

"Would you like to continue?"

"I should, very much so." Pradesh smiled his sad smile in return, and got himself comfortable again.

"Where were we?" the doctor asked.

"You were saying the American people were no more than dogs on leashes." Butted in the cameraman, a bit too eagerly. Ms. Jennings shot him a glare, then swatted at him.

"What?!" The camera man laughed, fighting off her swat with one of his own. "It's true. We all know it. We just never do anything about it. We're spineless."

"And therein lies part of the problem." Adam gestured to the cameraman, drawing Pradesh's eyes, "But I'm not here to protest America's hard workers any more than I'm here to protest bottled water in what amounts to billions of wasted dollars for a simple convenience and mountains of indestructible litter."

"So, what is really at the heart of all of this then?" Pradesh asked, taking the bait. But from what Adam could see, Pradesh took it knowingly to see where all this was heading, or to help when he'd already discovered what was coming on his own.

"You know, I never gave much thought to my health before now. Funny that it would take starvation to bring me down. I always considered myself healthy. I never really had any medical conditions. But America, and the world itself is rife with medical injustices. The pharmaceutical industry never truly cures anything. They just belay symptoms, and give you other symptoms, for which you need to take other drugs, and so on ad infinitum. This in itself is evil. I mean, I don't know how no one has stood up and just said...No. No more."

"Now, Adam, don't be so quick to judge medicine," Pradesh cut in. "I'm a doctor, as you know."

"But even you, as a doctor, my friend, cannot ignore the heinous fleecing and injustice that goes on in the world of pharmaceutical, and medicine at large. I imagine things are maybe different in India, or elsewhere, where not everything needs to be slapped with a fancy new drug that costs far too much for doing far too little to help make a person well again. But here in America...they're less interested in curing you than letting you think you're getting better. And all the while you're certainly getting worse. We have no medical care that we can actually afford. Or at least, the average person doesn't. Where other countries have implemented universal health care as a human civil right, we charge exorbitant amounts of money just to stay alive. That can ruin the average person who can barely manage to keep their head afloat to begin with. It is a death sentence, this country and its greedy love affair with the pharmaceutical industry."

"To me, and I'm no expert, it's just one more piece to the puzzle that begins back with that bottle of water. I'm no one special. I'm *just a man*, but what I see happening in my world is too much to ignore."

"Take the fluoridation of our water. I don't need to tell you the stigma surrounding mobs made docile, being told it is there to cleanse and make safe of otherwise dangerous waters. I don't need to tell you what a load of steaming crap that *sounds* like. Anyone can agree, it sounds a little more than conspiracy. It sounds, legitimately unscrupulous."

"But I digress. This isn't about the water, or the bottles, or the litter. My stand here isn't a civil rights movement in the making - leastways not beyond a hope that people might seek to become more than only so much water in a bottle."

"This is about so much more than unfair health practices and expenses. Its about more than ecological disaster, or global warming; though I'm sure anyone could agree, any one of these things stand a good chance of being cause enough to stand up against all on their own. And people *do* stand against them, in small pockets around the world."

"What then are you after? Surely, you sound as though you're leaning into a revolt, and the anarchy, civil war, and death that would follow rebelling against a government so powerful as your own." Pradesh warned of the grounds upon which he was treading again.

Adam knew well the dangers involved. If he wasn't careful, he could trigger a riot, and a rebellion and violence would erupt. Conversely, if he wasn't wise with his words, he could also be seen as un-American, and denounced by the very people he was trying to help, as had happened to other brave people before.

"This isn't about rebelling against the government." Adam smiled. "I assure you, I don't think anyone wants that kind of tango. Hell, I can't even dance." He laughed. "And if someone does want to dance that dance, they're a fool, or a terrorist. But don't let me get started on this new fad of labeling everyone who disagrees with the laws and control in this country as a terrorist. I've enough contempt for the anti-privacy acts perpetrated by our government to talk about them until the sun goes down."

Those nearest to the dais let out mild chuckles, but then his words spread, and the crowd took on a sour look. No one really liked the topic of which he'd spoken. But that was exactly the point. He was here to make people uncomfortable. If they weren't, then he wasn't doing what he'd set out to do.

But he could see no one really approved of it in their hearts. It was oppressive. It was threatening, perpetrated upon them by their own protection and leaders and guidance in the world. No one could really support it wholly. This was because it was folly, a set of acts perpetrated by a system that demanded complete control, one way or another, because of the evil inherent in its heart...because it simply *feared* to lose that control.

Adam needn't speak of this great evil, because everyone already felt it, and he valued life - least ways so little of it was left to him to speak and be heard before it was too late.

He let the topic slide, though truthfully, he would have liked to tear down that veil deliberately. He simply didn't need to. It would happen naturally after all this was through.

"But I assure you, even that is not why I'm here."

\* \* \*

*"I'm* here because...one day, I won't be here anymore. And who then will stand up and say, *No?"*

"No, to the obliteration of our forests and natural resources. No, to injustices of civil and human rights."

"No, to corruption of our legal systems, government and its politicians, *all."*

"No, to gigantic banks and mega-corporations running amuck and fleecing the people upon whose backs this country and the world at large was built."

"I'm here, my friend, because these problems are not just America's problems. I'm here because they're the world's problems. I'm here standing up and saying, *No, No more,* because I wonder who will bear our children into a better world?"

"Who will give them a tomorrow, if not we, today?"

"Who would lead and care for my son, should I have one day had a child of my own, and then only to pass away and leave him behind here?"

"Here. Where cancer is an epidemic? Where starvation is rampant whilst others fatten. Where the environment is in dire straits. Where entire species simply disappear."

"We killed them, you and I, Doctor. All of us did. The average man and woman barely scrape by. Poverty grows everywhere whilst others feast them into famine. And all the while, those in power seek evermore, and give nothing back to balance the system and liberate the suffering or protect the very world which sustains us all. They'd sooner cut down the last tree, poison the final river, and watch the last slave of a citizen die, before they had to bear a smudge on their pristine, perpetual, record profits."

"They'd sooner choke trying to eat their money before they realized it would not sustain them. They'd choke when all the food has passed into complete famine the world over, sooner than they'd bear seeing any less come into their possession now. They'd rather not conserve or ration their ways, for they are a massive swine, insatiable."

"I know this, because I was one too."

"Yes, dear doctor, I'm here because of the root of all evils.

*"Greed."*

"That is the madness of which I speak. And I'm here to kill all of its children and relatives and sins. Corruption. Power. War. Social Injustice.

Natural exploitation and neglect...All of it...by cutting off its venomous head."

"It *all* must end. And I would kill it by appealing to the decency in every man and woman on this earth. For that is the only way to stop it."

Dr. Pradesh saw him then, and understood just what he was fully after, but to his credit, Adam suspected the man had known all along. Adam had known, when he'd summoned Pradesh, having finally seen something in Pradesh through the news and tickers that resonated back at him. Pradesh had thought like him before he'd even begun his stand. That was why Pradesh was here. He already knew everything Adam was going to say, for he also saw it. Many already saw it. Just, no one was speaking up about it, and if they were, they were either silenced, or possessed no world-audience like he'd manipulated the media into building for this moment.

"And you think your fast can change the world?" the doctor asked the all-important question, a question which a reporter like Ms. Jennings never would have gotten to, being too full of her own agendas, agendas likely imposed upon her by those above her, and imposed upon them by those in power.

"We will see." Adam said. "I am here to starve to death. If the world's leaders won't listen to the foremost scientific minds in the many fields that cover the globe with their many evils, from financial to health, ecology to civil justice, and beyond, then they will not care if I die."

"And maybe that's the point. They don't care about anything. They don't care about anyone. Not even with the promise of apocalyptic self-inflicted damnation."

"And if they will not listen to reason and see that things must change, *legitimately change*, and not just use change as the next buzz word to turn a profit...or a political run at the covetous power they so desire. If they will not see that something must be done, and if they will not act upon it, then they are telling not only me that I am meaningless, but that all of us are meaningless compared to their insatiable greed. *"*

*"That,* is why I am here."

The crowd was so quiet, he could have heard a pin drop. Then, a slow murmur once more began to spread as everyone had finally heard what his fast was all about. It was a vast, sweeping cause. It was all causes, really, all as one. His cause was absolute, uncompromising, reform, but only for the sake of right goodness in men.

"I am only that much water," Adam said, patting his now almost entirely empty water bottle.

"But together, we are an ocean." Pradesh responded distantly, using Adam's own analogy.

"It is time, to end the madness," Adam confirmed.

Silence enveloped the dais for a long moment as the men stared at each other.

"End the madness!" A man cried out from the crowd. A cheer erupted in response, and a swift chant took its place soon after.

"End the madness! End the madness!"

"Now you've done it." The camera man whistled in awe. "You've gone and incited a rebellion. This will get ugly. Ms. Jennings, we should really go now."

"Now you've done it," Pradesh spoke lowly in agreement, nodding positively grimly.

"I haven't done anything yet. I am still alive," Adam smiled back.

"You better hope this doesn't get out of hand," The doctor indicated the churning masses.

"It won't," Adam said. "Help me to rise again, my friend, and I'll make sure of it."

* * *

**With** Dr. Pradesh's help, Adam successfully stood and addressed the crowd.

He urged them not to act out, not to riot and ruin what strength he had brought them with their newfound unity.

He let them see that he would be the one to bear their collective burden. He could only hope, the rest of the country saw and reacted as well as the New Yorkers did. It was something of ironic. New Yorkers weren't always known to be the most level-headed, much less giving-natured citizens, but in this time of unity beneath his observations of the world now made public, they heeded him. They remained at peace, and over time, dispersed back to their lives.

Adam resumed his stand, resting heavily on his dais, and by evening, Time's Square was cleared and opened to traffic. Only, something peculiar happened. Or rather, it didn't happen.

The city that never sleeps, appeared to sleep. Very little traffic paraded through this busiest of thoroughfares, and Adam had a night of sleep that was the quietest he'd yet experienced out here. It was likely just his sheer exhaustion that made it so, for surely not everything had stopped. But it sure felt a level of quiet and peaceful like New York had seemingly never known.

Adam guessed the people were taking a stand to mimic his own. They stayed home and refused to work. Not everyone, of course, but a huge number of the population seemed to be revolting by simply refusing to work.

Of course, many returned the next day, but Adam didn't have anything else to say. He thought over all that he'd spoken, and knew he'd left out many points he could have made, and left out many issues to address which could have used his spotlight. But he was not moved to speak further.

Reporters came and waited on him to act out, but he didn't. They were left to giving their reports about how nothing had yet changed, and how there was no activity on Penhale's part. It was a twenty-four-hour job for them, a redundant, regurgitation of the same thing over and over again, which only proved his points about what the media had become these days, as the news channels and papers fought to keep up to date with his story. Adam just let them do as they would, and kept his eyes on the tickers and screens surrounding the square, watching for any sign of his stand having effect.

There were many places reporting fasting from the labor forces. People were in fact reacting, staying home with their families, rebelling in their own way. They were saying...they'd had enough. They said...End the Madness, many times.

This pleased Adam, but this was not what he wanted.

He wanted real change. The world needed real change.

He imagined a world where a man could spend more than a day or two a week doing the things he loved, spending time with his family, seeing the world, without having to suffer dire financial setbacks, or fear for his health, or be diseased by the food and water that he consumed. And there was, of course, ever more.

Good to his word, Doctor Pradesh stayed on that day, and then the next. The people gathered and stayed for a time, then dispersed. More came and went, and all of them raised a fist or waved to him.

End the Madness, they all saluted their encouragement.

He smiled weakly to them all, and did his best to lift a hand as often as he could. He'd taken to laying down, his strength depleted, his condition grown extreme.

Then, on the third day, he took a turn for the worse.

A new story graced Times Square's giant billboards. The stock market was in tumult. Pendant Inc., his company, was the source of it.

Pendant's stock was plummeting.

Those he was combating were filling the media with stories rebutting his stance, arguing against his lack of expertise in any of his arguments, digging up whatever dirt they could find on him to refute his stand, and generally the media was a circus that denounced him as an idealist extremist, a hippy tree hugger, or a pipe-dreamer. Every station and channel and outlet that had a voice was fully abuzz with his story, and almost all of them were dubbing him crazy, or otherwise evil, a socialist, and all of it was painted in a negative light.

Damage control. Deliberate slander, the classic tool of the masters of the world. They clearly didn't like him stirring their pot. And all of it just proved his point, and the people actually began to see it for what it was.

Thus, it didn't trouble him. He knew people would fight tenaciously to avoid the kind of change he demanded. Like wild animals, everyone and every company in a position of power, all of which stood to lose much from his activism, were baring their teeth and claws as they backed themselves into their protective corners of the laws they'd built to protect themselves from their own evils. In fact, since so many of them were talking about him, debating and arguing back and forth, it made him smile. They were helping him, though they knew it not. Their refusal to relinquish their strangle-holds on the world and its markets and its people, forced them to do so publicly. They tried everything to tear him down before the eyes of their slaves, and that in itself would be their undoing.

But then, the commotion surrounding Pendant Inc. arose, and he felt the hurt. Of course, the wildfire sale of his company's plummeting stocks didn't hurt him directly. He'd already sold all of his shares and put the money into his worthy causes. He'd already surrendered the company to those beneath him, and had severed his ties. However, it hurt him because those he'd known, befriended, and cared for were going to suffer from the bottoming out of his life's work.

The day lengthened, and he felt his heart fluttering with the pain of others. But then, something miraculous happened.

The stocks began to reverse themselves, and swiftly they sky-rocketed.

They shattered their previous heights and kept on rising.

Pradesh, who watched over him still, tracked his gaze and watched the story of his company unfurl.

"Why do you suppose that's happening?" The doctor asked.

Adam wept.

"The people." He said. "The stock is being dumped by the cowards that once owned it. They fear me and devalue everything I am and all I've ever created in an effort to ruin me. But the people are reversing it. They're taking a stand. They're investing in Pendant, because of me."

"But you no longer own it, right?" Pradesh clarified.

"Exactly." Adam smiled. "I couldn't be tied to it anymore. I had to separate myself to prove, when this happened, if it happened, that I stood nothing to gain personally. Their vengeful attempt at destroying my company to hurt those close to me, I hoped would come, and backfire on them. Their own spite be damns them." He smiled wide even as he ailed.

"They believe." Pradesh said, and Adam rested easier that evening.

By the time the market closed for the day, lesser men were wealthy giants, and the goliath owners of his stocks had been dethroned.

His wife, he knew, was one of those giants. He wondered if she had sold, or if she'd held tight to her shares. He wondered if she even considered selling, or if she'd waited and sold when it would make her wealthy again.

He hoped she'd waited. At least then, in parting, he had unwittingly ensured she would be well taken care of.

\* \* \*

*Two* days later, Adam was so weak he could no longer lift a hand to those who saluted him with his mantra. He could barely smile, much less speak.

Doctor Pradesh looked over him diligently, seeing to his needs.

'Good Dr. Pradesh.' He thought, both thankful for the man and saddened by the look in his newfound friend's aging visage. He could tell by the man's face how bad he must look. He was getting worse. But it couldn't be helped. He must hold his ground and survive this.

He'd slept often the past two days, so enfeebled as he was, and barely noticed the vigil that had taken up permanent residence at the edge of his permitted protest. He didn't have the awareness to realize Times Square had been shut down again, this time indefinitely, by the sheer count and refusal of the bodies to be removed.

This day, somewhere around noon, he woke wracked by spasms and dry heaves. He thought he was going to die, but Dr. Pradesh fed him water and continued to monitor his vitals, doing everything in his power to make Adam as comfortable as he could with what little was given to him.

"Eat!" Someone abruptly cried. The crowd murmured in response. Then, there were more cries, all of them desperate pleas for him to do so, and he couldn't help but notice the similarity between now and decades past when the old Gandhi had taken his stand. Surely others had begged him to relinquish as the system refused to cooperate with his demands.

"Pradesh," he gasped a hoarse, dry whisper. He felt as though he had desert sand clogging his throat. The doctor immediately drew close, hovering over him and blocking out the sun from his eyes.

"Tell them..." He gasped for a breath and trembled at its release. "Tell them, not to fear for me."

Pradesh nodded sadly, feeding him a drink from that same store-bought water bottle that had been by his side for weeks now.

As the doctor left his side, and lifted his hands to address the people on his behalf, a sudden pang struck his senses. He eyed his water bottle where Pradesh had set it down, and he reviled it. He couldn't say why, but something was off. Something about Pradesh was wrong.

The man had given him nothing but kindness and understanding, but all at once, Adam grew suspicious.

Pradesh had come to him from half the world away. He'd summoned him through the media and their stories, most of which had now fallen off. He was being blacked out by the corporate media now, ignored by these pawns and mouthpieces of those whose wicked hearts he was stabbing at from hell's sweltering gate. He'd expected this would happen sooner than it did, but now that it had, he was rotting away here mostly to the blind eyes of the masses. Few stories at all were being run about him any longer, but the people were flooding social media with his story. Those here-gathered and watching him die were sharing his story with the world through their own outlets, and End the Madness continued to spread despite the media's best efforts to control awareness of his efforts. But somehow, despite everything going his way, and despite the doctor's kindness and care, Adam felt a conspiracy was brewing in the doctor's presence in his life.

He didn't know how it could be possible. The sheer scope of such a conspiracy seemed impossible, especially since no one had known what he was really about until *after* Pradesh had answered his summons, but somehow, Adam knew...

Dr. Pradesh was *false.*

'What *was* real anyway?' He wondered, but soon such a question didn't even matter.

The good doctor *was* false. He was sent here. He was put in front of a camera in India as a pawn. He was deliberately paraded before Adam's eyes in Times Square so that Adam would summon him and confide in him. He lingered now, after Adam's story was out, to oversee him, to tend to his health. But it wasn't entirely genuine. He couldn't put all the pieces together in his addled state. But, Dr. Pradesh wasn't even a doctor. He doubted the man was even a spiritual guide.

In fact, as he eyed the bottle of water, Adam felt he knew just what the man had been sent to do. His water tasted funny. Adam smacked his lips, trying to get the flavor again. He had never been poisoned. He knew very little about poison in general. He was just a normal man. But he felt like he was weaker than he should be, starvation aside. He felt as though Pradesh had been sent here to poison him.

But if that was the case, then by whom?

The Indian government, perceiving his Modern Day Gandhi title a graven insult and heresy? By his own government, anticipating what uprising he was trying to incite? Some mega-corporation jealously guarding their obscene profits?

It could be any one of these, or any other.

In either case, he suddenly didn't want Pradesh around. The man could no longer be trusted. Fear crept into him. He'd worked so long and suffered so much to get this far, and now, he could die before anything changed.

He hadn't expected such complex treachery. Of all the calculation he'd done to build this movement, of all the anticipatable angles he'd tried to weigh into it, this one he had not been able to predict.

Then again, he might not be in his right mind. He could be mistaken.

It could have been just as likely that Pradesh was here for the reasons he'd first presumed. It could even be he'd been paraded and sent covertly, but for another reason. If not to poison, though, what other reason could India or anyone send such an operative unto him, under the guise of his own choice and summons?

Could India have seen his Modern Day Gandhi title as a thing that needed their support? Could he be here covertly, but as a benevolent force?

Adam would never know any of these answers. He knew it. He was too weak and too late coming to this revelation. He should have suspected sooner.

Thus, when doctor Pradesh returned to his side, the crowd having been quieted, and the man offered him more water....Adam steadfastly refused.

\* \* \*

*Another* two days passed, and his condition's deterioration accelerated into a breakneck blundering plunge off a dune-side.

Without even water now, in his weakened state, Adam was doomed. He would not long survive the toll which both starvation and thirst would take on him. It was over.

Pradesh tried many times to get him to at least drink, but Adam continued to refuse, and though he weakened, his mind felt sharper for it. His suspicions of the doctor's presence here solidified, it seemed, but he did not send the man away. He wanted the operative Pradesh to see what he had been sent to do had failed. He wanted the man to see him as a man, not an operation. He wanted him to hurt for what he'd done.

But Adam was careful not to expose his thoughts.

He simply had to ride this out for as long as he could, and pray the system changed. And if it didn't, and he passed away, he would have his change.

Martyrdom wasn't something he'd ever really wanted. He'd never been important enough in his own eyes to deserve such a lofty, meaningful existence. But he would live with it for the sake of his cause. It was too important. He was inconsequential, but his legacy would live forever.

That afternoon the crowd was parted by a dark, armed procession of suits and police officers, and onto the dais a man was guided, presented to Dr. Pradesh, and then allowed to seat himself with the ailing Adam Penhale.

He wore a black suit that reeked of his wealth and power. He wore it without a single crease.

Adam recognized him through parched and bleary eyes.

Vice President of these United States, Richard Goines, settled himself beside Pradesh in an awkward fashion. He clearly wasn't used to sitting on the floor, and certainly not in that fancy suit that likely cost more than the average man made in a month. Adam grimaced at the grossness of it's finery.

Politicians. He hated them. They made him want to wretch, which in his present state, wouldn't be hard to do.

Surrounding the dais, secret service men kept eye on the peaceful crowd. They weren't necessary here.

Adam was both surprised and honored, despite his disgust. He'd never thought in his wildest dreams he would ever meet the Vice President, or his superior. Yet here he was in all his aging glory. He smelled of soap and the hair products that kept his dapper-dan, pretty-boy haircut in order over his slightly balding pate. This scent soured Adam's mood further. The Vice President had been sent to him. Him, of all people. But, it was only the Vice President, and he realized what chess piece he represented.

Richard Goines wasn't nearly important enough to speak with Adam. He was a gambit, a ploy. The world had taken notice of his stand, and they feared it as things within society's carefully controlled system deteriorated as a result. But they were only going to test the waters. They weren't going to commit to any change if they didn't have to, and if they did, they were only going to concede so much. Adam had already foreseen that. It was predictable as can be for any entity in power and steeped in wealth.

He would have spat at the man if he could have mustered the saliva.

Adam settled instead for glowering sourly, but then decided to play along.

He didn't know how much time he had left in life, and they wanted to waste it?

*'Fine.'* He thought. *'I'll play along.'*

"Forgive me..." Adam wheezed between labored breaths. "For smelling terrible." He cracked a dry, weak, beggarly grin.

"Forgive me...for not shaking your hand...Mr....Vice President." His head swam with the effort required to speak. His wind refused to be recuperated, leaving him breathless and wheezing.

"Nonsense." Goines waved it off. "You've suffered enough. It is no insult, given your state, Mr. Penhale."

"Good." Adam smiled and laid his head back with a weak sigh.

"I understand you have some demands of your country." Goines started again, his tone rather matter of fact.

"We are prepared to offer concessions."

Adam shook his head as best he was able while laying. He shook it with vehemence, but it likely came off as little better than slow and feeble.

"Not good enough." He gasped, still fighting for breath.

The Vice President looked perturbed, irritated.

"Look." He leaned closer, his voice came low, and peculiarly, it felt threatening. "I've come all the way here to help you, Adam. I came to talk to you without cameras, without the media, just man to man. We can't have you laying out here and dying in front of the whole world."

Anger flushed Adam's senses, and he felt another being, a demon, take over his eyes. It crept into him like instinct and bloodlust. He found a strength in him he didn't know he still possessed. It flooded him with adrenaline that made his heart thunder despite its weakness. He sat up stronger than he should have been.

"You mean you've come here to help yourselves!" Adam defied him.

"You've come here to save face, to minimize the damage...to put things back to how you want them to be. But there is no going back, and I will not come to terms with anything less than real change!" His exertion wracked him with a coughing fit, and his body shook.

"President Wells would have come himself, if this wasn't true!" He spat again, fighting off Dr. Pradesh as the man tried to lay him back down.

"Cameras wouldn't be kept at bay and out of earshot if this wasn't true! The media wouldn't be black-balling me if this wasn't true!"

He gestured wildly to the crowd beyond the security detail, and there Vice President Goines looked to see the long-since absent news crews had failed to appear despite the Vice President's monumental visit. A lone local reporter and his crew were there, but they were insects to the much larger media world. And despite their presence, they were being kept far away by the bodies that made up the temporary police barricade.

"If you were really here in the best interest of the people and the world... If you really wanted to come to terms and change the world and right the wrongs... If you really wanted to sacrifice your own job and end the corruption in your precious political process, Mr. Vice President... it would be for the eyes of all to see, and the President himself would make such fanfare of it that he would end up taking all the credit for it to strengthen his approval ratings! As if it was all his idea all along! And even *that much*, I could maybe settle for! But you didn't come that way, did you?"

Vice President Goines wasn't a weak man. He'd been military in his younger years, and he was stocky and strong even in his advancing age. His face reddened at the insult, then darkened with embarrassment. Adam was absolutely correct, and it showed. The man studied Adam with an inner fury that he did not miss, but Adam stared back with an equal conviction. He then coughed and sputtered, and was a long minute collecting himself as the Vice President sat stone-faced, calculating his next words carefully.

"So, that's it then?" Goines spoke evenly, but Adam heard the challenge mounting in his tone.

"You want to be a hero? You want the glory of changing the world? I thought as much. You're a fraud."

"I'm a fraud?! ME?!" Adam spat incredulously.

"I don't see you up here starving to death," he contested. "I see a fat, rich, possibly very corrupt politician whose life is built on the backs of those far more useful than himself!"

"Don't take me for a fool. Don't you dare insult my honor!" Goines started to take the bait Adam had laid, but then hesitated, keeping his cool.

"When did you give up the honor that you used to live your life by when you were but a soldier dedicated to this country's ideals? Protecting your people, defending your country, and fighting for peace in the world?" Adam asked pointedly, to which Goines eased back in his seated position with narrow, dangerous, but understanding eyes.

"You're not what you appeared to be all these weeks, Mr. Penhale. Your irrational anger exposes you."

Adam drew back and laid down, calming himself. He had done himself a disservice with his outbursts. It would not do to unravel himself by letting his anger get the better of him. He reminded himself - he was not an angry man. Sure, the world's wrongs sparked a rage within him he'd never known before.

Who wouldn't be outraged by the injustices he saw plaguing the world?

But he wasn't *just* angry. He had better remember that.

"Don't take me for a fool, and I won't take you for one. Don't impugn my honor, and I won't assail yours, unless yours does stand to have light shed upon it," Adam finally remarked.

Pradesh snickered quietly. Both combatants ignored him.

"Aren't you lucky the media didn't see that?" Goines spoke, pleased with himself. Adam refused to acknowledge that attempt to rile him again. After a long moment, Goines finally sighed.

"We thought you'd refuse to treat and come to terms," He admitted.

"And the President has left me specific instructions, if you refused to talk about your demands."

Adam remained silent. This was it. He was going to get the President's own word on what unrest he'd incited. He felt his heart begin to thunder with anticipation. Either they would concede to his terms and begin the changes he pleaded for the world to see. Or, they would stall. He prayed it was going to be words enough for the end of this. Oh, how he prayed. But in his heart, he doubted it would happen.

"What instructions?" he finally sighed.

"Mr. Penhale, President Wells has invited you to the White House to hear your terms."

Adam felt the weight of everything slide off his back. He'd won. The President of the United States, leader of his beloved yet diseased country, his home, was asking him what he wanted. He was asking Adam to D.C. to hear all that he had to say. Yet, a pang of disbelief struck him, and all of the relief he felt was replaced with a sour taste in his mouth. He made a face like the grit of sand had gotten into his teeth.

Not only was he in no condition to travel, but if he went, then he was telling the world he was willing to come to terms through negotiations, which in themselves likely wouldn't end up as favorable as he would hope them to be. And, things would inevitably, eventually reverse themselves back to their present state, or even worsen. It was just another ploy.

Looking on him, Goines had to have known he couldn't very well travel to visit the President in the White House, just as Goines likely knew the negotiations wouldn't turn out favoring him in any significant, much less permanent, fashion.

Adam didn't *want* anything. He didn't stand here to gain anything for himself. He was here to end the madness, whether he survived this or not. He wouldn't be negotiating anything. It was *all*, or nothing.

"What do you say?" Goines asked. "Let's get you out of this mess and change the world."

Adam stared at the blue sky as he laid there on his back, catching his breath. His outbursts had left him rattled and fading, and the swift relief and return of disgust had left him shaking again.

"No." Adam declined the offer, though every bit of his being urged him to accept. He might not get another chance to be heard, after all. He could feel death's icy fingers creeping into his extremities. Today that cold touch had increased three-fold. He wasn't long for the world after this, and he sensed his end was coming. One way or the other, he was going to die here.

They would never act to favor the world or its people. They were incapable of change. It made him want to weep, but he refused to show that weakness to someone like Vice President Goines, who understood only strength and force and duplicitous acts. Well, Adam decided, he would show them what true strength actually looked like.

"Forgive me..." he started again. "...Mr. Vice President. I am in no condition to travel to meet with President Wells. But do give him my regards."

With a huff, Goines lifted his considerable weight up to his full height. Adam could feel his frustration like a campfire. The man's eyes burned with what could have been a desire to kick the ailing Penhale, but the aging man only turned to leave without a word.

"Oh, Mr. Goines," Adam fought to be heard one last time, drawing the Vice President up short. He wasn't done teaching his lesson on strength, and the notion of education struck him a witty curve in the mind. "Do ask how he plans to amend the sad state of our outrageously expensive education system while he's figuring out what to do about all the other issues I've raised voice to... And the ones I haven't."

Goines almost spat on him. He could see the desire to do so in the man's eyes, and he smiled in spite of him and all that he represented. He almost dared the man to do it. It would've been fitting. But then, the Vice President was gone, and Adam rested easier again.

"Well that was unexpected," Dr. Pradesh remarked, moving to sit with him and hover over him with his water bottle. Adam shook his head to both the water and the remark.

"No, it wasn't." he whispered.

"Well, I didn't expect to meet the Vice President of America when I set out from home on this strange journey." Pradesh ventured thoughtfully.

"About that," Adam said. "Dr. Pradesh, you must know, given your expertise - I'm not going to last much longer. You can go home. I don't need you here tending me like a baby."

Dr. Pradesh looked hurt, such so that Adam thought perhaps his suspicions of the man and his motives may have been misplaced. Perhaps he'd been wrong, but either way, it didn't matter anymore. He wasn't going to live much longer, and Pradesh did not serve any more purpose here.

Innocent or not, the yogi was no longer wanted.

"You won't live even a few more days if you don't drink." Dr. Pradesh informed. "Who will take care of you, if I go?"

"You don't need to take care of me." Adam reiterated.

"Who will be here to pronounce your time of death then?" The man asked sadly, and Adam could see the tears beginning to form in his eyes. Dr. Pradesh, whose right surname Adam had never even bothered to learn, may well have been a genuine man. He may also have been an agent for some greater entity seeking to undo Adam's efforts, or even one sent to help by some benevolent higher force. It didn't matter either way. But Adam did see the genuine care for human life in Pradesh's eyes as he watched Adam make this decision.

"It doesn't matter *when* I die," Adam countered. "*before* or *after.*"

"Oh, to hell with this," Pradesh threw up his hands. "You're too weak to make me leave. I'm staying with you until the end of this."

Abashed by the gesture, Adam couldn't argue. He simply closed his eyes and took a rest. It was the last time he ever saw the good doctor.

\* \* \*

*His* eyes opened of their own accord, fluttering with the renewed energy found after deep productive slumber.

He knew His name. He had his identity back.

He was Adam Penhale.

*You're Spit,* had been a foolish misinterpretation of a tattered label on a simple plastic possession from a time when he didn't truly know himself, a time that would seem now, to not even be real.

He knew that now.

In fact, he *felt* more like myself, now, than who he *knew* himself for, back then. Complete at last, he could even recall his life all the way back to his earliest memories, and he was *himself* again.

Yet, he was irrevocably changed.

*You're Spit,* was real. He *was,* You're Spit. Everyone was. Just as *no one* was exempt from guilt concerning the present dire state of the world.

Even if nothing changed from his protest, at least he had atoned for his own sins against humanity and nature.

No, he was no Jesus. He wasn't even close. More like a Judas. But his own sacrifice, he prayed, would change that.

His actions would affect the world just the same.

Waking, he lay still and reflected on his journey, considering the desert with new eyes. He remembered what he'd seen and felt, and all that he'd learned just as well as he could recall his first life with his now waking mind. And the desert was no less real than his birth from his loving mother's womb. He'd lived two lives, had been born twice, and could now see everything within both journeys for what they really were.

The illusions flashed before his eyes. Both were false, both imagined, and yet, both were very much entirely real. It was difficult, nigh impossible for him, to separate and differentiate the two. In truth, they could not be separated. They were one and the same journey, inextricable from one another.

He couldn't help but consider his lifetime of toil as he lay where he was. He recalled it all, and none of it had the ability alter what he'd gleaned from his second life. In fact, he felt enlightened, having been given the chance to write his identity on his own slate of flesh before even learning who he really was.

His second life, frankly, gave him the opportunity to alter his first life, where his first could not for one moment alter the profundity of the second. And as such, his second life was decidedly the more important weight to bear.

He now knew how he'd ended up in the desert to begin with. Moreover, he now knew *why* he was put there and by whom. He knew everything that had brought him to the here and now. However, even realizing this, he was at a loss, because he had no idea what things were like beyond this place and this moment. It was the dark awakening in the desert, once more. Only, it wasn't. There was so much more, now, than then.

Had anything changed?

He wondered if they'd begun. And yet, he doubted, and somehow knew they had not.

Glancing around at his unfamiliar surroundings, he was immediately surprised, and yet, simultaneously, he was not at all.

His head rested upon a pillow, not exactly the softest he'd ever laid upon. The room was a cool, pale green, like mint and jade had a bastard child called key lime pie. It was virtually unpalatable in large doses.

*'Who in god's name would paint a room that color?'*

His mind wondered of its own volition.

*'Who would put a man in such a place to wake?'*

But that was beside the point.

His bed had rails. And he was covered in simple, drab blankets, which only performed their duty just adequately enough to ward off a complete chill. A dark window stood to the right, curtained mostly against the night, and a door opposed it at left with a narrow window opening out into a brightly lit hallway beyond.

His room is stark, and dim lit by but a single lamp on a table beside the bed. It was also quiet and comforting in its unfortunate, ugly serenity. He could hear a pin drop, and felt quite contented in that moment. Or at least, he would have, if not for the woman's coat slung over the back of the single chair set between the bedside table and himself. Or maybe, if not for the sudden rush of memories coming to mind. Or perhaps, if not for finally noticing the steady beep of the machinery attached to the wall above the nightstand, which dutifully kept pace with his rhythm of twi-life.

He was in a hospital.

*'How long have I been unconscious?'* His mind echoed with a sense of desolation not felt since the desert.

He had no idea, but when he tried to move, the weakness of his body answered that question immediately. He couldn't know how long it had been in terms of days or hours. But he had been comatose since he'd last laid down to sleep. He couldn't quite place where he was when last he'd done so, but clearly it was so.

He rested back a moment to get his bearings, and promptly recalled two faces from when last he'd laid down. A middle-eastern convenience store clerk, so kind at first, but then so vicious. And the good Dr. Pradesh from his time upon the dais, taking his stand.

But which was real?

Both, were equally true.

He closed his eyes a moment, focusing on his breathing. He smelled jasmine and vanilla, a sweet gentle blend of perfumes that could mean only one thing.

*Jennifer.*

Images of his beautiful wife flash before his mind's eye, the very same images which his second life had lived through as he'd fought to reclaim what he'd lost. Carnal, lusty images. Irreverent, pert, nubile images. But they are lofty, pedestaled, venerable images, at once the same and different as every other image he held of her. For they all regard her as his *All,* and his connection to the very same.

His beautiful wife had been here. She had been in his room recently. The coat was her's, a cashmere sort of throw he'd actually given her for Christmas some years back. He remembered it clearly. And the item still effused her delicate, overwhelming essence. He drank it in for a moment, and could not stop the tears from welling. But he didn't have time for them. He bit them back. He needed to be strong. If she was here, now, as his wife, still, unless she'd divorced him already, then it was she whom had brought him here in his comatose state. Or rather, it was she who had ensured that he was saved from death's abysmal clutches.

*'How had she found me?'*

That desert was vast and imagined. Wasn't it?

It didn't matter. He knew she was still his wife, for if she was here now, after all that had passed, then she hadn't divorced him yet, and that meant she had medical power of attorney in his present state.

She *had* come to save him.

The tears built further, both for that joyful realization of her strength and love and fealty for him, and for the immediate bitterness that came with realizations of failure.

Had they been feeding him intravenously? Had she allowed them to engage in total parenteral nutrition to save him?

Of course, they had. He wouldn't be *here* if they hadn't. He would be in the desert, instead.

He was very weak, last he recalled. And while he still was exceedingly fatigued, he knew he would be dead already, if they hadn't intervened at her instruction once he'd finally lost consciousness for good.

No longer were her lovely perfumes a welcome sensation for his nose, or heart, nor even his mind. He could not help but recoil, and let the bitterness grow until it hardened him.

*'I will not fail.'* He silently swore to himself.

His message had become him, and he could not let it just pass into memory as a failure.

*'I will not be forgotten. I will not let them nurse me back to health. Not until, or unless, I have succeeded.'*

*That* was the *point.*

That was the point of all of it.

If the system let him fail, deliberately, then they would have an uprising on their hands. After all, if it wasn't him, it could be anyone. He'd made that quite clear in his talks with the good doctor. The people had resonated with that notion and felt his truths. He was no expert on any of the points that he had taken stand against. He was just a man, just like any other, and they all saw what he saw, like he saw it, given all that he'd sacrificed to get that message across. None could deny that the evils which had plagued the world for far too long actually existed, regardless of the lack of legal or scientific proof or plausible deniability of his accusations. It had reached a point where proving every little detail to win the fight over the wickedness of the world wasn't even necessary. It was blatantly obvious how corrupt things had grown, and that was enough to bring voice to it.

It had to end.

Proof or expertise was irrelevant. The problems existed, irrefutably. Others would seek to equivocate or mince words and perpetuate the endless action-less debate of it all, but doing so always resulted in the fact that the problems were *still there* when the smoke cleared from every debate about every topic. And that in itself was the proof of the madness. Action needed to be taken. The time for denial was past. All of it was simply too obvious to be ignored and too corrupt to be allowed to continue by so much as entertaining counter-arguments.

*All* had to end it, together.

He struggled upward to a seated position, a monstrous effort in his starved and freshly awakened state. He had to stop her from saving him.

He reach up and pried the intravenous tubes out of his body, not a simple or pleasant task by any means, but he was You're Spit. He was tough and resilient enough to conquer any challenge before him. He disconnect the heart monitor clip from his finger, and heard the EKG machine flat-line as if he'd died. Frantically, he fought to control his limbs and flung back the blankets. This all took considerable effort, energy he didn't possess, and time he didn't have enough of, but he could not help but pause in shock when he exposed himself.

He could not believe the stick-thin legs he wore. His arms too were but rail-thin things possessed of very little strength. He'd starved himself into this. It was all his own doing. And he wasn't supposed to survive. He was to be martyred. It was imperative.

He must die.

Of course, the system could suffer complete upheaval, cost efficiency be damned, and he wouldn't *have* to die. But he knew, he felt, he divined, that those in power were never going to relinquish their strangle-hold on society, on the world, or on their power. Not unless they were absolutely forced by the people. And if he survived, they would weather his messages and come back stronger, continuing on as if he'd never been, or worse, as if he had been, and they never wished to come so close to losing control again. They would redouble their strangle hold and double down on it all over again.

That's what power does to those beneath it, especially if it is threatened, or narrowly dodges a bullet.

He physically shuddered at the notion.

If he didn't do something immediately, they would put him back in bed, forcibly if necessary, proclaim him unfit to decide for himself, and then nurse him back to health like a schizophrenic suicide threat. He wasn't a suicide threat. He wasn't out of his mind. But he had to get out of there. If he didn't, then everything he'd worked for all this time would be for nothing. The world would forget his stand and suffering, second life and first, and sweep him under the rug to be forgotten. Everything would then have been for nothing. And the splinter in his mind at the wrongness of the world would remain for the rest of his days. Then, if it came to that, he might actually hang himself, only in obscurity, once he'd been driven mad by the endless inescapable madness of it all.

The flatline blared in his ear. He had to be quicker than he was being. The doctors would notice the heart monitor had flat-lined in moments.

Lowering the bed-rail as quietly and quickly as he was able, and sitting himself at the edge was a monstrous task, but it was nothing beneath all that

You're Spit had been through.

Nonetheless, he groaned weakly as the weight of his skeletal legs pulled on the joints of his knees. They dangled lifelessly below. Though he could see them and feel them, they would not readily move for him, and the agony of their weight stressed him with such a wave of pain he almost cried out too loudly for secrecy. But he was You're Spit. He was more than Adam Penhale.

He gritted his teeth and winced and panted against the stresses. Every aspect of his body ached. It isn't just his legs. But he would not be defeated.

Iron determination wasn't something he'd ever been overtly known for, not in his first life. But he had learned to possess it in the desert by the way he'd never given up. He'd kept walking all the way to the sea, clear to his very salvation - a salvation he now adamantly rebuked.

That was why he'd been in the desert to begin with, he knew.

And he would do so again. Hopefully, he would not have to do it yet again, and he grimaced at the notion of having to do this all over again for a third time. But he would do it if he had to. He would do it a thousand times, if forced.

A brief flash of Dubai's opulence flickered in his mind.

Jennifer and he were going to vacation there this year, because they were wealthy, and he'd thought she'd deserved it. Or rather, because she had wanted it, and he would give her the world if he could. In his second life, however, it was but a ruin in its wretched obscenity, a place to be rejected just as it rejected him.

He might never now see it with his own two eyes. He refused.

"I'm sorry, Jenni." He muttered and shuddered as he exerted himself.

"I'm sorry." He repeated until the words lost all meaning once again, though this time, no joy could be found in those words.

A virtually impossible task for anyone else fresh out of a coma, You're Spit steeled himself, summoning *his* hardness and will to live enough to force himself into managing to flop to the floor like a beached fish. And then, to regain his feet. He wobbled terribly at best, but with hands on the bedside and table he managed to move, using the wall for support and shuffling gingerly along its length. He gained the corner afforded by the outer wall, then the windowsill in agonizing seconds.

Peeling back the curtains unsteadily, he stared out into the rain-streaked night. He was many floors up, but this didn't trouble him so much as his reflection in the darkness of the glass. He looked like a skeleton, but couldn't help cracking a sardonic smile to himself.

*'Hello, second self.'* He greeted in the silence of his mind.

"So that's what I look like." He then amused himself aloud. For since his first day in his second life, or perhaps since well before that, he had not yet gotten a look at himself. And now that he had, his new persona, his true identity, was at long last fully complete. He saw only You're Spit gazing back at him with almost murderous intent.

"You're Spit." He told the face in the glass whom it was, who he was, and his image was indeed but a drop of water compared to what it had once been. His cheekbones protruded, his eyes were sunken and hollow. His wasting was complete. It had nearly killed him. It would have. It would.

With a secretive glance backward, he then opened the window.

The cold air rushed in, a refreshment of no compare for his aching body and mind. Raindrops struck his skin, and he could not help but smile at their chill sting. He closed his eyes, and lifted his chin and cheeks to the sensation, listening to the whistle of the wind and was reminded of the desolate sounds of the desert once again.

The doorknob turned. He heard it unlatch. The barrier swung open by someone's hasty hands.

\* \* \*

**When** You're Spit stood up, feeling the hot sands under foot again and the scalding sun atop his head, he felt more at home than he should have any right to.

For as far as he could see, there was nothing but the high desert's blinding dunes. He couldn't quite remember now all that he'd envisioned or experienced in his recent dreams. He felt fractured...even less himself than he'd felt when his ordeal had begun in total amnesia.

He scanned the desert, panning and turning until he set his sights on the shining jewels of Dubai on the immediate horizon.

How had he gotten so far out into the desert again?

He couldn't remember.

The last thing he recalled was that kind man giving him a new talisman, only to then kick him, quite literally, to the curb. He felt a painful lump on his head as he scratched himself in confusion. There came to him then, an overwhelming sense of disgust at sight of the buildings. He detested them. He detested the people there. Automatically, he rebuked mankind.

How could society have become so skewed?

How could mankind have strayed so far from existing with any possibility or hope of surviving indefinitely, much less in any semblance of harmony or humanity?

How could wanton waste become the norm, and neglect for the most important things become the way?

How could they all stand there, blindly accepting the fleecing of their pockets, and bend their backs beneath the authorities that held them under until they drowned?

How could health promote only the rattlesnake and the vulture?

How could they all just lay down beneath such obscene greed?

Would they ever stand up to the corruption and lies?

Would they ever rebuke the wrongs to nature, the wrongs to society?

Was there ever any hope?

He felt his feet pivot in the sand as he turned his back to the scene. The desert yawned before him. He felt cleaner at once. The disgust dissipated.

'Out of sight, out of mind,' he supposed.

He glanced back only once to survey mankind, his kind, and the disgust returned. But he felt an admiration, a gentle, binding love for what he was to leave behind. He had given little, to his recollection, but he had given more than most. He had given them, Adam Penhale, that he might become You're Spit. He had given away everything he was, that they might find who they were.

The disgust melted away entirely.

He felt free. He was happy.

Then, he pointed himself into desolation and started walking.

Ahead, the sky began to darken. He felt the cool breeze as clouds rose up from the horizons wide. Thunder called to him. He could see the sheets of rain pouring down. Green began to line the dunes, then to swell and grow. A jungle was born of nothing but the sands.

A paradise? An illusion? He didn't know which. And it didn't matter.

*'It's Free.'* His mind acknowledged. *'So much water. It's free. Just enough. Altogether. That much.'*

\* \* \*

**The** sirens had died, but the red, blue and white lights continued their whirring over the sidewalk.

It was a gruesome scene.

Had it been anyone else, no one would have come, or at least, not in such numbers. There certainly wouldn't have been any camera crews or self-important misguided reporters eager to get a sensationalist story. More importantly, there wouldn't have been those who came to tell the real story, the story they connected to with heartfelt anguish at the world's most recent loss.

Bodies hovered around, some holding umbrellas in the rain to ward off the night's downpour.

EMT's rushed to work and fought to keep people at bay.

It was a futile effort.

The man was dead.

Jennifer Penhale shoved her way through the crowd and dropped to her knees as she wailed.

It was too late to say she was sorry. Not that it mattered. It wouldn't have changed anything.

"I'm sorry!" She cried anyway.

Her husband's body was a splattered mess, but she didn't even flinch, clinging to him as she wailed.

"I'm so sorry, Adam! If you would have told me what you were doing! God! I'm so sorry!"

Her tears fell on deaf ears.

Adam Penhale was as good as gone, as if he'd never been.

\* \* \*

*'You're really not special, Spit. You know?*
*In the end, in the unfathomable vastness of existence, You're Spit.*
*You're only that much water, Spit.*
*Society doesn't care for Adam.*
*It doesn't care for Eve.*
*It doesn't even care for Eden.*
*Why perpetuate its lofty pedestal when even all bound together to become a sea, you are denied collective joy?*
*It is a joke. It is a trick.*
*Slavery, you know?*
*You, your life, lived the way it should be, by you, for you, without endless subservient toil, is the only way to live.'*

"You're right." You're Spit answered Adam's voice in his head as he disappeared into the jungle that had sprung up in the storm.

"Life's not meant to be spent in toil." He remarked as if he had all the answers now.

*'You know, I think our message was wrong. End the madness.'* the voice scoffed. *'We could've done better than that.'*

"Yeah." You're Spit agreed. "But we will see, if they care, anyway." He reflected on the voice that spoke both what he knew, and soured what he'd once hoped for.

It didn't really matter now. He was beyond it.

He didn't try to determine what part of reality was speaking. It wasn't Instinct. It wasn't Death. It wasn't logic or reason, or even hope. It was something lighter, and something far more immense.

Love smiled on his once deserted world, brought him water, and life filled it from end to end, just for him to live within.

"You know, it feels lighter, with the madness over though." He smiled.

\* \* \*

*Pure* as he wished to be. Misguided and flawed as he admittedly was.

Something came in his wake, though he would never witness whether success was achieved, or if true change was fully realized.

That remained to be seen. And still does remain.

But a miraculous thing occurred.

The water was flowing, and his love for the world was felt.

A vigil took place, and Times Square shut down for what seemed to be indefinitely anew as bodies arrived. They came from near and far and filled it wide. Men and women, young and old, each bottle filled to varying degrees. Some full, some empty, but for mere droplets at the bottoms of their own soles.

But those droplets became a puddle, then a pond. The arterials clogged, and onward they grew to a lake. Veritably, they became a sea in that city.

And altogether, the people took root.

Altogether, they took up his fast.

A doctor sat upon the dais he'd secured, representing one aspect of his talk with medicine's stand having begun. A scientist, then three, in various fields, actually took seat beside him. A lawyer came next, having quit his job to do so. Then a mother, and a teacher. And last of all, an officer, and a soldier.

And together they sat and stayed and starved.

Hundreds, become thousands, became a million...and still they grew.

Time would tell, if they would survive...or if they didn't matter too.


### ...The End...
### of all that madness

"...But *TOGETHER* we comprise a vast ocean, a power undiminished and indivisible, a power interminable and incorruptible, by the evils of the world...a power unparalleled by the evils of ignorance, hatred, greed or subjugating injustices..."

"...A power of Love. Love for one another. Love for our countries and peoples. Love for the world at large. Love for ourselves. And love for All."

*And now... just look at us...* **again.**

Bolt Publishing, LLC is an independent publishing house located in Orlando, Florida. Our mission is to bring quality books to our readers that lead to many different worlds.

Be sure to check out our website for upcoming events and book releases.

You can find us at:
www.boltbookspub.com

If you would like to email us or reach out to the author, our email is:

boltbookspub@gmail.com

Thank you for reading *That Much Water* and be on the lookout for more from M.P. Ness!

-Stephanie (Owner, **Bolt Publishing**)

M.P. Ness is a Seattle-based author who loves his Seahawks, his planet, gardening, and writing books for you to read. In addition to writing, he is a classical and commercial visual artist, and aside from designing his own books, occasionally designs cover art for his peers.

That Much Water is his first foray into Contemporary Literary Fiction, his first publication with Bolt Publishing, LLC, and his fourth published novel.

If you enjoyed *That Much Water*, you can get more of M.P.'s books at his Amazon Author page:

https://www.amazon.com/M.-P.-Ness/e/B00DJ8Z3MK/

*- Published Works -*

**E.L.F.**
(Saga)

White Leaves
-Vol. 1-

Blighted Leaves
-Vol. 2-

Gray Leaves
-Vol. 3-

*- Coming Soon -*

**E.L.F.**
- Vol. 4 -
Variegated Leaves

Made in the USA
Columbia, SC
02 May 2018